& Vixens

I0592526

Kim Petersen

Cataloguing-in-Publication entry is available from the National Library of Australia: http://catalogue.nla.gov.au/

Title: Angels & Vixens

Author:Petersen, Kim (1973 -)
ISBNs: 978 – 0 – 6481595 – 0 – 6

Edited by Paul Vander Loos, paulvanderloos.wixsite.com/editor
Cover layout by Paradox Book Design
Interior Design: Champagne Book Design

For the sea, the mountains and the ever-changing
drifting clouds.
You are more than inspiration.

"I am the enlightening, revealing presence, manifest with full power"
—Jesus the Christ

Prologue

June 10, 1998

Dear Journal,

Almost every night he appears in my dreams. First, he smiles at me under the shine of the sun. The revelation that sparkles in his eyes show me the love that I know still flows through him. I always smile back and call to him. But he never comes. Instead, he turns away from my pleas and goes to the shade of the avocado tree. I notice a deep hole in the earth and I beg him to step away, for somehow, I know the pit is filled with something sinister. His blue eyes darken like a raging sea and ___ me forever. He steps into the hole, I cannot ___ and call for my brother ... Ace, where are you?

I begin to stir; my sleep becomes restless and just before I wake I catch another glimpse of him. I catch the twist. I feel his blackened heart turn to ash as his lips glint with the smile of a large serpent. His lidless eyes curve with the flash of sapphire. Then I know he is lost to me.

Will he ever return from the dark force that consumes him?

All I know is, I have to find a way to help him.

Millie xo

Chapter One

MILLIE HELD THE END OF THE PAINT BRUSH between loose fingers as she cast her eyes on the bare canvas in front of her. Her lips parted as they curved into a smile. 'Faith,' she whispered before closing her eyes. Her breath slowed to a rhythmic draw as she centred herself within her consciousness and a ball of sapphire light began to assemble above her head. 'Faith,' she said again. The ball of blue light sparkled and amassed as it hovered over her as if she wore a shining halo. The glowing sphere began to descend, and as she took her next breath, it infiltrated itself through the crown of her head.

Millie felt the tingling warmth of the ray seep through her mind, and she could sense every inch of its movement as the faith-light-ray filled her being and twisted through her. Her smile was one of contentment as she was overcome with the feelings of unity and protection that faith evoked in her. She opened her eyes slowly, and when she looked to the blank canvas before her, this time she saw the vibrant colours that would shade it into a painting of another world. She turned to the stereo near to her and hit the play button, then leaned to dip her brush into the palette. 'Hello, faith!' she said, as her hand flew into a painting frenzy.

'Where do I find this world?' Millie said over her shoulder as she worked.

She felt a slight tingle breeze over the back of her neck.

'You can find it from within, Millie.' Samantha's voice echoed around her.

She paused for a moment. 'Hmmm … do you know this world?' she asked.

'It is a world for the ascended. But it is a world that any being can visit, earthly or otherwise.'

'How do I know that I'm painting it right? I don't even know this world,' Millie mumbled with a shake of her dark ponytail.

Samantha laughed gently. 'There is no wrong way to portray this world, Millie. It is a world of individual creation; purely thought-created.'

'Oh. That sounds interesting,' she said.

'It is a world beyond even your most wild imaginations.'

Millie turned to peer behind her just in time to catch the dissolving image of coloured wings. She grinned. 'Bye mamma.'

Two hours had passed in a flash while she granulated a combination of siennas, ivories and ultramarines against the canvas. Pausing to survey her work, she reached for the gold leaf to accentuate the sunlight that beamed over the long slants of the pyramids she had painted when she heard the footsteps and laughter of Craig and Arella as they scampered their way into the workshop at the back of Holly's gallery.

'Mummy!' Arella burst through the door and ran into her arms.

Millie chuckled. 'Well hello butterfly.' She bent down to kiss Arella's nose. 'How was school today?'

'Oh, well,' Arella took a deep breath and her eyes widened. 'We did another lesson on the alphabet this afternoon. Miss Graham asked us to write down every letter of the alphabet and make a sentence using three words that she had written on the chalkboard – fox, brown and quick. So I did, but when I told her that my sentence used every letter of the alphabet, I think she got a bit cross with me.'

Millie glanced at Craig before looking back to Arella. 'Why? What sentence did you write down?'

'The quick brown fox jumps over the lazy dog,' she said as she began to rummage through her school bag. 'Amy and Jade said my sentence was dumb.' She rolled her eyes as she handed Millie an envelope.

'Well I think your sentence was very clever, never

3

mind Amy and Jade,' Millie took the envelope. 'What's this?'

'It's from Miss Graham. Am I in trouble, mummy?' Her aquamarine eyes looked worried before they clouded over as she gazed at the canvas behind Millie. 'Oh Mummy!' she gushed, 'It's the Golden World. How did you do that? Have you been there?'

'No, have you?' Millie asked.

Arella's dark ponytail bounced at her waist as she nodded. 'I go there all the time. You should come with me one day!'

Millie laughed and rested her stained fingernails on Arella's shoulders. 'I would love that. But you'll have to show me how to get there, okay?'

'Sure, but we can't get there together. We can only meet there.' She looked at the canvas thoughtfully. 'We can meet at the unicorn gates, that's where I meet Sammy sometimes … except, I can't see them on your painting yet.' She paused to take a quick breath. 'Can I go see Aunty Holly now? She promised me ice-cream.' Arella beamed.

'Of course, butterfly.'

Arella skipped over to the door before turning back to Millie. 'By the way, grandpa will be here soon, and his heart is racing and racing,' she said, then disappeared through the threshold.

Millie raised her eyebrows at Craig with a grin. 'Hi,'

she smiled with an audible sigh.

'Well, hello,' Craig beamed. 'Finally, we can greet!' he chuckled.

He leaned forward to brush his lips on the cheek she offered.

'Hmmm … it can be difficult!' She regarded the clock on the wall in mockery. 'I think we made for good time today all things considering.'

Craig laughed. 'You mean, all-Arella considering,' he said and turned his attention to the canvas. 'The Golden World, hey?'

She followed his gaze. 'I suppose it is …' she turned to him. 'How does it make you feel?'

Craig looked at the painting for a few minutes before turning back to her. 'Like there is nothing in the world to worry about. It makes me feel at ease. Completely, utterly and wonderfully at ease.' Whiskey coloured eyes glowed as he shook his head slowly. 'How do you do that?'

Millie's heart fluttered as she held his gaze. 'I'm not really sure,' she shrugged, tearing her eyes away. *Better not to get lost in that pot of honey*, she thought. She turned from his stare and began to fumble with the envelope Arella had given her. 'Thanks for picking Arella up from school today,' she said.

'Any time. Can we have dinner together tonight?'

She drew her eyes from the letter and glanced at him. 'Craig,' she pleaded.

'Just dinner, Millie.' He grinned and curled a lock of brown hair behind his ear. 'No funny business, I promise.'

She sighed. 'Hmmm … I am pretty hungry,' she admitted. *Why is it so damn hard to resist him?*

'It's a date then,' he teased.

'Craig!' she pouted.

'Hey, hey! It's all good. I'll pick you and Arella up at 6 o'clock,' he laughed, turning away and heading for the door. 'But you know I'll never stop until my ring is back on your finger,' he added before disappearing through the door.

Teeth twisted over her bottom lip. 'That's what worries me,' she muttered under her breath.

She turned her attention to the envelope and pulled out the letter from Arella's teacher. She smiled as she read the note explaining that it would be to her daughter's advantage to skip a grade; apparently kindergarten didn't sufficiently challenge Arella. 'Trouble indeed,' she murmured, reaching for the gold leaf to resume her work on the canvas.

As Millie worked, her thoughts mulled over her relationship with Craig. Since Damon had reappeared in her life, she found herself torn between her love and loyalty for Craig and the overwhelming feelings that bubbled to the surface for Damon. She had no choice but to break off her engagement to Craig until she could figure out where her heart really belonged. What she hadn't expected, however, was Craig's determined presence to continue in her life. He had been hurt by her decision, yet despite her protests, he vowed to remain close to her and Arella until she made a choice. *A choice that is becoming near impossible,* she thought with a frown as she smeared and blended her canvas.

A sudden knock at the door startled her.

'Millie-pie? Can I come in?'

Millie turned to face Damon while she wearily pushed a wisp of hair back from her forehead. *Oh no!* Her mind spun in an instant jumble as she remembered Arella was in the shopfront with Holly. She had been successful in keeping her relationship with Damon on a strict business diet for the past six months; he and Arella were yet to meet. For now, she'd like to keep it that way. *At least until I find the courage to tell him they shared a daughter.*

'Sure. Hi Damon,' she smiled as he gingerly walked into the studio.

'I'm sorry for interrupting,' he smiled apologetically. He frisked his long fingers together and breathed into them. 'It's getting cold out there.'

'Yeah, maybe you should invest in gloves. Did you come through the gallery?' she asked.

His brows creased. 'Uh … no, I came through the alley gate. I called earlier, Holly said you'd be out here. Is there a problem?'

Her shoulders relaxed. 'Nope,' she said.

He held her gaze as he closed in on her. Invading her space as he reached across and gently wiped the smudge of paint she had smeared across her forehead. 'You have paint on your face,' he murmured.

Millie's eyes dropped to study his lips only inches from her own. Her heart quickened when she felt the shallow warmth of his breath sweep across her face. Catching her own breath, she stiffened as she tried to ignore the tingle his touch provoked in her.

'Oh,' she laughed, pulling away and rubbing at her forehead with a rag she pulled from the pocket of her overalls.

Blue-lagoon eyes watched her with the swim of amusement.

He cleared his throat. 'I have some news,' he said, smiling as she continued scrubbing randomly at her face.

Breathe! She turned her now blotchy forehead from him and made for a nearby stool. 'Oh?' She perched and tried to appear casual.

Damon fought to hide his grin. 'I have just finished with a phone conference with *New World Art* magazine. They would love to run a centrepiece on you, Millie … and the best part is, you will be featured on the cover of their September 1998 issue!' he grinned.

Her heart skipped a beat and her eyes widened in

disbelief. 'What? Really, Damon?' she murmured.

'Yep,' he smiled, watching her carefully.

Her lips curved into a wide smile as she digested the information. 'How did you manage this? *New World Art* is the most prestigious art magazine in the world!' The pitch of her voice elevated.

He laughed. 'I know.'

She rose to feet and threw herself towards him. 'Oh my god!' she squealed.

He caught her in his arms, slightly lifting her weight in a half-twirl while they laughed together.

Millie closed her eyes against his shoulder, and relaxed in his embrace. When she caught his sensual woody scent, she pulled away abruptly. 'How did you do this?'

His fingertips lingered on her waist until she moved from his grasp. 'It's all you, Millie. Your work speaks for itself,' he said.

She grinned at him. 'Thank you, Damon.'

He grinned back. 'They'll be sending someone to Australia to interview you and take photos of your work. And of course, this will probably mean a trip to New York will be on the cards for us soon, so get your passport ready,' he said.

She clutched the side of her head and gave another squeal. 'New York! Oh, how glamorous.'

Her eyes dreamily darted to the ceiling as she

contemplated. 'I've always wanted to go to New York,' she smiled whimsically. 'Wait … Why are we going to New York?'

'I am currently setting up deals with some art dealers and collectors from across the US. When this issue is released, interest will swell. That will be the time to jump. You and your work will be hot-to-trot.'

His eyes trailed to her neckline where they rested on the diamond crusted half heart that dangled above her cleavage. 'It's not enough to view your art. They're like hungry sharks keen for the next kill; they'll want flesh and blood. They'll want you.' The blue in his eyes deepened. 'Something I'm all too familiar with.'

Millie ignored the flip of her heart as her fingers grasped at the long ends of her ponytail. 'Umm … sure. Well, I guess we'll being going to New York soon,' she mumbled, fingers tangled in her hair.

Damon's eyes flickered with amusement. 'Old habits die hard, hey?' he said.

'What do you mean?'

He gestured towards her twirling fingers. 'Will you bring Arella? If we go to New York? It would be nice to actually meet your daughter,' he said.

Millie lurched from the stool. 'I don't know,' she muttered. 'Listen, I have to get going in a sec. Thanks for stopping by with the great news.' She hurried for the door.

Damon hesitated. 'I was hoping to take you to dinner tonight to celebrate. There is a new seafood restaurant in town. I hear the lobster is delicious,' he winked.

She smiled as her eyes met his in a moment of memory: her eighteenth birthday dinner when Ace had baulked at the lobster. 'I already have plans. Another time, perhaps,' she murmured, looking away.

He sighed. 'With Craig?'

'Yes, with Craig,' she snapped, suddenly annoyed. *What is it with these guys?*

His eyes brooded. 'Sure. Talk soon, Millie-pie.'

She began dimming the studio lights and screwing paint-filled lids onto their tubes. She grinned to herself as she thought about her art gracing the cover of such a reputable art magazine. Damon sure had lived up to his word. He had worked tirelessly for the past months on a marketing plan for her art, and all that hard work was beginning to pay off. She had been selling many pieces and could hardly keep up with the increasing demand for her paintings. It all seemed to be falling into place. She frowned. She wasn't sure how or when to tell Damon and Arella of their kinship. She knew once Damon was aware Arella was his daughter, everything would change. She just wasn't sure she was ready for that. Her eyes fell to the floor in a moment of guilt; she knew she'd have to tell them soon.

She reached over to switch off the stereo, pausing

to gaze over her day's unfinished painting. 'The Golden World,' she said thoughtfully. 'Someday I will find you … or perhaps you will find me.'

Her head cocked as she heard the heavy fall of footsteps outside in the alley.

'Millie!' her father burst through the studio door with a loud thud. 'I'm glad you're here,' he said, panting.

'What is it, Dad?' her eyes scanned his ashen face.

He clutched one hand over his chest while flashing the other palm at her. 'It's Ace,' he gasped. 'I've heard from him, he just called the house.'

She frowned. 'What did he say? Where is he? Is he okay?' She tripped over her words while resting a hand on his shoulder. *He looks like he's going to have a heart attack!* 'Are you okay, dad? Come sit.'

Steering him to a stool, she waited with growing impatience while Glen's heaving chest subsided and he regained his breath.

His face was grim. 'I don't know where he is, he didn't say,' he rasped. His big head shook slowly and his bewildered eyes sparkled like a goldfish. 'His voice was tainted, Millie. Like it wasn't his own. I hardly recognised his voice.'

'What did he say?'

'He said, "I am becoming the serpent. I will sliver unnoticed among you all because I am the son of the serpent god and *she* has betrayed me",' Glen said.

'A threat?' She grasped at her ponytail.

Glen shook his head. The wrinkles on his face deepened. 'I don't know, it sounded as much. The thing is, he began to howl like a baby wolf pining for his mother. He cried like he was in pain. He can't control the serpent, Millie. I need to find him before it's too late.'

She reached for her father's hands. 'No, Dad. *We* need to find him. Is there anything else? Something that might help us find his whereabouts?'

'No. But somehow I don't think we need to worry about that.' He squeezed her hand. 'I think he's coming for you, Millie-pie.'

Arella looked up at Millie expectantly. 'So, I'm not in trouble with Miss Graham, mummy?'

'Not at all,' Millie laughed. She patted a hand on top of Arella's pillow. 'Lay down, butterfly.'

Arella threw herself backwards, landing in the folds of fluffy blankets and pillows. 'Then why do you look so worried tonight? Is it grandpa?' She propped herself up on one elbow.

Millie sighed. 'Have you brushed your teeth?'

'Yes.'

She leaned towards Arella. 'Breathe.'

Arella blew as hard as she could.

'Whoa!' Millie reeled back. 'Are you trying to blow me away, young lady?' she chuckled.

Arella giggled. 'Maybe just a little.'

'Oh yeah?' she teased, tickling Arella's tummy.

Millie murmured words of sweet dreams and love and kissed her daughter goodnight.

Arella called as Millie started to leave the room. 'Mummy, I'm going to sleep with one eye open like a dolphin.'

'Have you been reading uncle Ace's book of facts again?' Millie said.

Her dark head bopped. 'Uh-huh, it keeps him close to me.' Her little brows knitted under the dim glow of her room. 'Mummy, if you ever can't find me, make sure you meet me at the unicorn gates of the Golden World, okay.'

Millie frowned. 'Why would I never be able to find you, Rella?' she asked.

Arella shrugged. 'Sometimes I dream of a black snake.'

'A black snake?' Millie felt her chest tense while she sat back on the edge of the bed.

'Only sometimes. It's okay mummy, I don't think he wants to hurt me. I'm not afraid of him.'

She snuggled in her blankets and sleepy eyes drooped to a close.

'Good night, mummy,' she murmured.

Millie watched her sleeping daughter for moment. Her heart began to thump wildly as she rose to leave the room. Her face paled and she clasped a hand over her mouth as she ran for the bathroom. Overcome with feelings of anxiety, she could barely dislodge the lump in her throat. *He's coming for me*, she thought with a trace of despair. *My brother, my beautiful brother. How do I save you from yourself?*

Chapter Two

July 3, 1998

Dear Journal,

It is so easy for our thoughts to stir. The more we think on a subject, the more thoughts like them are added. It's not unlike making a soup; at least that's how I like to see it. We add a little worry here, a dash of anxiety there, mix in a whole lot of fright, and voila: we have created ourselves a simmering pot of revolving discord ready to generate the corresponding feelings. Only by then, those feelings may become too difficult to control.

Of course, the same can be said when we choose to make a soup of joy – but how many of us are actually so aware of the thoughts that are contributing to our soup? For our soup inevitably becomes our reality ... the cause in each individuals conscious creation.

I figure, if I can face this fact completely, I may be able to conquer myself.

I figure, if I can conquer myself, I may then be ready for the dark power of the black serpent when he calls upon me.

Lately, I have begun to speak to the God-self that lingers in my brother _ the unflawed soul I know lives beyond the serpent. And while I send a blended ray of gold and violet to him, I ask his divine self to accept the peaceful uplifting rays I shower over him. If only a spark infiltrates through the blackened shell that encases his heart, then I will consider my efforts sustained.

It is my greatest hope that over time the violet ray will dissolve the dark that has accumulated over him ...

If only he will listen ...

If only he will allow ...

Millie xo

The blues of his eyes reflected the blood-orange sky that soared over the slopes of the mountain ridges as he found a secluded place along the rocky stream that looped around the edge of the land he had been working. He had been ambling through Mary Valley country for the past months, finding work among the farmers that could use an extra hand on the land. Ace found that labouring land abundant with pineapples, macadamia nuts and livestock didn't pay nearly as much as he'd like. Yet each fleeting stint came with a bed and three meals each day; enough to bide him over until he was sure he had evolved his newfound skill enough to make his next move.

He sat along the edge of the billowing stream under a blanket of hugely dense trees and gazed towards the sunset while he thought of his sister and her meddling ways. He had dwelled long enough under the patio shadows the night he had lunged the switchblade into his mother to witness Millie's healing power. He vividly remembered the sharp twist of rage he felt when the coloured wings had receded to reveal Lilly take her first breath after her death.

His lips curved into a sneer as he ran a calloused hand over the short spike of his hair. Just like his dear sister, he had discovered he possessed a unique power too. And when he was certain he had cultivated it enough, he had plans for his life-saving sister.

Ace closed his eyes, deliberately pushing his thoughts from his mind. His ears pricked at the sound of the nearby cows mooing. His golden brows creased. 'Shut up!' he growled. 'Go away, stupid cows.'

A few big brown eyes turned to look at him, and they began to shift away as if they understood his command.

Ace chuckled while he watched them walk away, then settled back to close his eyes once more. A deep breath filled his lungs repeatedly as he allowed his body to relax. He sensed the lift of a familiar boost begin to elevate through him, and he welcomed the change he felt as he consciously focused himself out of the shell of his body. Hovering above his head, he marvelled at the feeling of limitlessness that overcame him. He knew he was invincible and he felt every inch of the dark power growing within him. From here, he could see everything, but he knew he wouldn't stay too long; not yet.

He began to fix his thoughts on the serpent that had spiralled its way into his life when he was a child. The more he thought about his old friend, the more he felt its force envelope him. He began to spin, slowly at first, until he gained momentum and almost lost control as the black serpent appeared before him in a misty clouded vision. Fangs revealed themselves when the serpent opened its mouth and inhaled the essence of Ace until he was all but consumed. Totally within the confines of the scaly snake now, Ace looked down to his slumbering body below, and with the greatest of intention he focused himself downward. He entered through the top of his dense shell, feeling a sharp rush of pain as his outer body transformed and he again became aware of the hindrances that it brought.

He lay still under the shadows of the trees while he adjusted to an acute dance of vibrations that rang through his ears. He narrowed his eyes towards the mulling cows in the nearby paddock. A long forked tongue protruded over pointed white fangs as he gathered the odour of the cows, sending the information back into his mouth where he tasted their scent. He became aware of the hunger their essence had stirred within him, and briefly contemplated a rare-meaty meal. *Later*, he thought, as scaly black muscles moved and flexed. He set off towards the rodeo he knew most of the town-folk would be attending that night. *First, it is time to play*, he mused. After all, how else would he perfect his new skills?

Ace paused to linger behind a dusty old truck parked behind a crowded grandstand that overlooked the arena.

His eyes darted excitably to the people that had turned up in droves to watch cowboys attempt the most dangerous eight seconds in sport – bull riding. The crowd cheered and clapped, and there was an electrified thrill reverberating among the small horde while they watched a bucking young cowboy try his hand at the timed event. A loud horn sounded over the noise, signalling the end of the eight seconds, and the cowboy swung himself off the jerking bull with the aid of a bullfighting clown.

He slithered under the truck and glided noiselessly under the elevated bleachers, gazing up towards the treads and kicking of feet as they stomped and meandered over the wooded structure. His eyes widened as he savoured the mixed scent of sweat, assorted fragrances and beer that exuded from the crowd above him. Every one of his senses appeared magnified, and he could hardly contain the thrill that pulsated through his thick, long body. He moved closer to a sneakered foot that dangled down through the rafters. *Oh … anyone of them are so close to their death*, he relished, as he slowly licked the back of the dangling foot with his tongue. He manoeuvred his forked tongue with deliberate pace over a sock, until the taste of warm flesh sent an exquisite rush of hunger through him. He rose and arched the length of his upper body as he drew back ready to strike, the glint of teeth glimmered in the shadows.

A movement in the shadows caught his attention.

21

'Hello big black snake.'

Ace slung around towards the small voice to spy a little girl. She was kneeling at the side of the bleachers, staring at him with wide brown eyes. The ends of her long dark hair swept through the dirt as she cocked her head to one side and smiled. 'What are you doing under here? Are you lost?' she said.

Ace was momentarily speechless as he considered her imposing presence.

She crouched further into the dirty gravel, and crawled a little way under the grandstand. 'My name is Skye. Don't be scared, snakey, I won't hurt you,' she said as she reached into her jacket pocket and pulled out a piece of musk candy. Saucer-eyes blinked as she stretched out her hand. 'Are you hungry?'

Ace shifted the scales of his body and began to slither closer to her. He reached her quickly and lifted his head to level with hers. 'I don't eat candy,' he hissed, tossing his head to knock the musk stick out of her hand.

Her bottom lip began to tremble as she gazed down at the dirt-covered candy. 'Hey! That was my last musk stick!' she cried.

Ace chuckled as she looked back at him with the threat of tears brimming in her eyes.

'Why are you so mean?' she accused.

'Why are you not scared of me?' he sneered.

'Because I don't want to be scared of you! You're just

a big fat meanie,' she wailed.

Ace drew himself high above her, puffing his chest and cinching his upper lips back in a ferocious display. 'Well, you should be afraid, little girl,' he jeered, 'because I am mean and I am going to hurt you.'

She gave a high-pitched scream while scampering back to avoid the strike of fangs as they tore through the space between them like a bolt of lightning. His strike was met with a mouth full of gritty dirt. Ace flicked his head around in time to catch sight of a man's hand tugging the girl from the shadows just in time.

Faded blue eyes peered under the grandstand. 'Snake!' the man's voice boomed.

A few men scrambled down the bleachers to join him.

'Where?'

'Under the grandstand! He tried to attack my girl; he's a big black bastard too.' The ageing man consoled his sobbing daughter. He gave her a gentle nudge. 'Go to your mother, Skye.'

The girl's father turned towards the carpark. 'I'll get my axe; watch out for him,' he instructed his friends before disappearing into the car lot.

Ace eyed the small cluster of legs assembling near the grandstand. *Shit!* he thought, looking towards the old truck for an escape. Before he could move, one man leaned to peer under the shadows where he still lingered. He reacted immediately, lunging the full force of his weight to sink razor sharp choppers into the flesh of his victim's face.

Teeth submerged and tore through skin easily, and despite the threat around him, Ace felt a ripple of excitement surge through him as he tasted the blood of a human for the first time in his metamorphosed embodiment. The man gurgled and grunted as he fell to the ground groping at the strong jaws that held him captive. His solid body began to convulse as Ace released a fatal current of venom into his bloodstream.

A thumping pound on his head forced Ace to release his victim. Lights blinded his vision as he squinted towards the heavy boot that clobbered him again. He shrunk back and reluctantly retreated into the shadows with the vibrational sounds of hysterical screams ringing through his ears. He made a fast dash to the cover of the old truck where he watched the panicking crowd for a moment as they ran about in a frenzy.

'Oh my god!' a woman shrieked.

'Is he alive?'

'Call an ambulance!'

People hovered over the injured man, his body shaking violently as he convulsed and foamed at the mouth.

'Did you see that snake? I've never seen anything like it.'

'The biggest snake I've ever seen.'

'A monster!' someone declared loudly over the commotion.

The little girl's father came running into sight with a long axe in his hand. 'Where did the snake go?' he bellowed, searching under the bleachers.

'He went that way, Warren.' A bulky man pointed towards the general direction of the old truck. Then he gestured to the axe in Warren's hand. 'Mate, I don't think this is a good idea right now. That snake is too big, even with that.'

Warren chuckled. 'I can handle a snake, Greggo,' he muttered, turning to head for the truck.

Ace sized up the axe-carrying man, while skimming his tongue over blood tinged fangs. His heart raced in anticipation as he considered quenching his growing thirst for blood before Warren was joined by a couple of blokes.

An ambulance whirled its way into the dusty car-park. While the would-be hunters were momentarily distracted by its screeching sirens, Ace took the opportunity to head for the cover of the nearby bush, leaving a thick, slithering track through the dirt in his wake. He prowled deeper into the dense camouflage the bush provided and settled behind the trunk of a fallen tree. He sneered as he heard his pursuers trekking cautiously through the outskirts of the bush, uncertain about venturing in any further in the darkness.

'He's gone, Warren; we'll never find him now!' A man's voice boomed.

Warren hesitated as he scanned over the shadows of the rural blades of grass that tangled around dry branches and chunky trees. He glanced towards his friend. 'Did you see that snake's eyes? They were as blue as the sky just before dark fall. That was no ordinary snake.' He shook his head.

The bulky man slapped Warren on the shoulders. 'He's a snake I'd rather not see again … C'mon, he's gone now; let's get out of here and see how Terry is doing.'

Warren hesitated before nodding. 'Okay,' he conceded, allowing his friend to steer him from the bush.

As the men retreated towards the rodeo ground, Ace peered over the big trunk and noticed Warren glancing over his shoulder into the darkness. He recognised the spark that flashed through the man's eyes. *Oh, such determination!* He jeered to himself, before nestling down to prepare for his shift back to human form. *There is more amusement to be had here tonight,* he sniggered.

He had noticed some men's clothes hanging over the back tray of a ute he had passed in the carpark earlier. He planned on snatching them up as fast as he could, before anyone noticed him strutting around butt naked. Then he would join the delightful commotion of the

crowd ... *And perhaps even meet Warren,* he grinned.

Ace coiled his thick long body into a black scaly bundle, carefully tucking his tail under his large head. He closed his eyes and inhaled deeply before finding his centre of consciousness. He pushed himself up and out of his reptile body, relishing the feelings of power that accompanied his elevation. Spinning now, he held clear the vision of his human form before his eyes and with one determined thrust, focused himself to embody the familiar figure once more. As he entered through the crown of the unmoving serpent, he accepted the surge of pain while the transformation became complete.

Ace fluttered his eyelids as he arose from his attained metamorphosis. As the dizziness in his head began to subside, he abruptly became aware of the chill around him. He drew his limbs closer. He rubbed his arms to keep warm as he considered his experience. He cursed silently to himself as the memory of missing his first target and eating dirt struck his ego. His head spun when he heard a deep chuckle emanating through the wooded foliage.

'Don't be too hard on yourself; for you are still learning. We are pleased,' the voiced hissed through the inky darkness.

Ace squinted and spotted two yellow eyes flashing through the trees. 'Who are you? Show yourself!' he demanded.

More chortling echoed around him. 'You already know me well, Ace. I've been with you for some time ... continue the path that beckons you, for all riches and power await you.'

The gnarly voice faded with the dissolve of the yellow eyes, leaving Ace alone.

He jumped to his feet and ran against the cold night, stopping when he reached the edge of the bush to peer into the dimly lit carpark. Satisfied the coast was clear, he bolted for the clothes that still hung over the tray of the ute and drew the fitted garments over himself as fast as his stiffening limbs would allow, finishing the dressing session with an old cougar-style hat before setting off towards the rodeo arena.

'A little tight don't you think?' a woman's voice filtered through the darkness.

Ace jerked around with surprise. 'Huh?' he uttered, stopping to face a young woman leaning against a bonnet of a parked car.

She was wearing a buttoned-up flannelette shirt over black jeans that strained against her plump figure. Her long curly red hair sprang and jutted wildly and appeared to be aflame under the glow of a lone light-post. Her face was as pale as milk and ghostly against the thick ring of charcoal she wore around her eyes.

She grinned as she took out a cigarette. 'The clothes you stole. It's not every day you see a man walking out of the bush butt naked. I'm almost convinced you are the result of a spell I recently cast,' she said, laughing and offering him a smoke.

He ignored her outstretched hand and allowed his eyes to drift over her as he sized her up.

'Who have you got back there?' she gestured towards the bush.

He shook his head. 'No-one is back there,' he said. Eyes as cold as icicles speared through her. 'Are you some kind of witch?' he asked with half-interest.

She shrugged and tucked the cigarettes away in her bag. 'What if I am?' she said, challenging his icy stare with her own. She shuddered visibly, and her eyes darted from him before she switched the conversation. 'You realise there is a monster snake on the loose,' she said.

He drove his eyes deeper into hers before twisting his head in a wicked grin. 'Yeah, I like snakes,' he said, finding it difficult to keep the amusement out of his voice.

'I like snakes too,' she murmured.

He turned away from her before continuing towards the rodeo.

'Hey!' she called.

He paused to look at her.

'I'm Madison,' she said, blowing a thick puff of smoke towards him.

'I don't care,' he grunted.

Madison smiled as she watched him walk away. 'Oh, you will, snake-man,' she said under her breath as she stamped the cigarette out. 'You will.'

She slung her bag around her shoulder and ambled off after him.

Chapter Three

ANNABELLA NARROWED HER GREEN EYES AS SHE forcefully threw a big chunk of clay against the wooden table top. She scooped up the damp clay to carefully inspect it for air bubbles before wedging it against the hard surface a few more times. When at last she was satisfied all traces of air had been eliminated, she grinned and perched on the small stool before the pottery wheel. She selected the appropriate sized bat for the wheel, and placed her wedged clay in the centre of the metal plate.

She closed her eyes. Filling her lungs with air, she pushed aside all the incessant thoughts that seemed to plague her recently, and granted herself relief from their suffocating web. With the warm rush of an exhale, she smiled behind closed lids and welcomed the tingles of another realm as she approached the gateway.

Tall golden gates swung open to allow her entry, and without hesitation Annabella drifted through and into the golden threads of love she had become accustomed to visiting. She was greeted by a dark angel – her angel. This was her place of growth and blossoming. In this world she became the full magnificence of her glory as she joyfully received her lessons.

Today, however, she was here for no particular lesson. She had travelled through the veil and came here to receive inspiration. Since the passing of her father, her mother had taken a turn for the worse and it wasn't long before she was diagnosed with an aggressive strain of stomach cancer. Annabella had come to this world today to ask for assistance in strengthening her divine healing rays before she qualified the vase she was about to sculpture for her sick mother, Rose.

'Bella. Welcome.' The angel's voice reverberated through her like a radiant beam of light.

Bella felt a great sense of ease as she basked under her angel's immersion.

'My mother's illness is worsening. I have come to ask for help,' she said.

'I know, Bella. Together, we will consciously qualify your vase with healing today, but I'm afraid we cannot alter your mother's will. Her health depends upon the consciousness she has of it, and the will she is free to manipulate.'

Bella drank in her features. Her long dark hair fell supple to the coloured wings that hovered and bobbed behind her as if with a life of their own, and her emerald eyes illuminated bright upon her hallowed face. She always wore white. A sheer white gown draped over the petite frame, and when she smiled, she felt the warmth of it seep right through to her core. Bella thought it to be the most elegant, bewitching smile she had ever seen.

Bella frowned. 'You mean she may want to die?' she asked. Even in this celestial world she could still feel the discord of that thought creep up on her.

The angel smiled. 'Bella, we never really die. We make transitions into other realms, other forms. Your mother will always be with you – in this world or the next – just like your father.'

Bella nodded. She had never gone further than a few strides past the golden gates. It wasn't that she didn't want to explore this world; she knew it was hers for the taking when she was ready. As it was, to dwell near the gates was enough for her for now. Her vision beheld shimmering waters in the distance. From her standpoint, the water appeared deeper and a richer blue than any stretch of water to be found on earth. A blue that burned within the depths of her soul's memory.

The angel turned and followed Bella's stare. 'What do you see, Bella?'

'I see beauty everywhere,' she whispered.

The angel swept her eyes over her like a feather dancing in the wind. 'It's time for us to go, Bella. Your sculpture awaits.' She grasped her slender fingers around

Bella's hand, and Bella felt an exquisite shiver envelope her.

Bella placed the hot mug of tea on the circular coffee table in front of the real estate agent. She lifted her eyes to meet his while the briefest of smiles appeared at the corners of her lips. 'Cookie?' she said, offering a plate of biscuits to him.

He shook his head and picked up the steaming mug before him. 'No thank you. Tea is just what I need, it's so cold out.' His gaze fell to the cold oil heater in the corner of the room.

Bella followed his gaze. 'Oh,' she laughed a little too loud. 'It's broken … we … I haven't got around to having it fixed yet.'

She squared her chin. She wasn't about to admit just how dire their financial situation was. Truth was, she struggled enough to pay the mortgage repayments and bills for the family home, and she couldn't afford the added expense of a new heater. Or even to repair this old dusty thing.

Mr Adams considered her with a sympathetic smile. 'Are you certain that you'd like to go ahead and list your home, Bella?' he said, regarding the quivering fingers

that rested in a tangle in her lap.

She could only nod. She had little choice now.

'And your mother? She is sure …?'

Bella swallowed and breathed in deep, trying to curb the irritation that began to creep up on her. She cleared her throat. 'Mr Adams,' she began.

'Craig,' he interjected with a grin.

'Craig, my mother and I have discussed this thoroughly. We cannot continue the upkeep of our house on the small wages I draw from working at the aquatic centre. Medical bills are piling up … and that is only just the start. Should I go on?' the pitch of her voice raised a notch as she fought hard to hold back the tears that threatened to spill. *There, I said it!* she thought glumly.

Craig looked down into his own tea. He encircled the length of his long fingers around the hot mug as if the steaming ceramic cup might be enough to keep the chill from invading his bones. He nodded slowly and looked up. 'I'm sorry,' his voice faltered. 'Would you like to show me around the property now?'

When they rose, his tall figure towered over her like a willowy tree. *I feel like a weed next to this guy*, Bella mused, while leading him through the urban terraced house that rested snug between its neighbouring counterparts. As she reached the only bedroom she had ever known, a wave of nostalgia flooded over her. She was going to miss this house. Her parents had moved into the townhouse shortly before she was born. 'A new home for a new baby,' they'd often chirp when reminiscing. She had spent hours finding hiding spots between the nooks and crannies of the three-storey dwelling so she would be fully prepared when her best friend, Emma, would come to play.

She sighed heavily as her eyes lingered over the ornate Victorian styled cornices that decorated her bedroom ceiling.

Craig took in the timber four-post bed and the matching pieces of furniture that housed a cluttering stash of handcrafted sculptures. 'So graceful and elegant.' He gestured towards the vast space.

She wrapped her arms around her chest, clutching her knitted cardigan tightly around herself as she beheld the swirls and contours of white ceiling roses.

'They were my inspiration,' she said, gesturing to the roses. Her smile was whimsical as she twisted the ends of her honey-blonde hair.

Craig tamed a long brown curl behind his ear and watched her closely. 'Inspiration for what?' he said.

Her smile broadened. 'I'll show you,' she said.

She snapped around on her heels and headed for the door where she paused long enough to glance over her shoulder to him. 'C'mon, this way. To the best part of this house!'

She led him outside and under grey clouds that

hung gaunt and threatening over a small courtyard. They followed a moss-filled pavement that weaved to its end before a miniature cottage. Bella opened the door and stood back to allow him to enter first. She noticed the deep intake of breath he drew when he took in his surroundings.

'Wow, Bella! These are all yours?' he asked while taking tentative steps closer to the rowed shelves of sculptures. He spun around to look at her, yet when he spoke it was almost to himself. 'And the sculptures in your bedroom ...'

There were angels upon angels upon more angels; each one of them unique. Their features and wings were painstakingly etched in detail and painted with the tips of fine brushes. Some were elegant and mystical, others chubby and cheeky looking – all lovingly created and breathtaking.

Bella caught the ends of her hair in a twist. 'Yeah,' she mumbled. Not many people had seen her work.

Craig looked impressed. 'All of this seems so familiar to me ... you seem familiar to me,' he said absently.

Her brows pleated. 'Ummm ... in what way?' she said.

He shook his head with a quick squeeze of his eyes. 'The angels ... You.' He studied her for a long moment before the smile appeared again. 'Never mind. Do you display these in a gallery?' he said.

'Uh, no. I don't show them to anyone. I'm not sure they are quite good enough.' She walked deeper into the small room and perched on the pottery stool.

'Oh, they are good enough, Bella,' he said. 'Tell you what, I might know a place that may be interested in your sculptures. Would you like me to make some enquires?'

Her face brightened. 'A gallery?'

'Yep,' he nodded.

'Oh ...' She hesitated and looked at her angels. 'I'm not sure. Can I give it some thought?'

His eyes rested on a stash of empty chocolate bar wrappers littering the far corner of the bench top. 'Sure ... chocolate addiction, huh?'

A smile bloomed over her face. 'I confess,' she laughed.

He reached into a deep pocket of his trench coat and pulled out a chocolate bar. 'Me too,' he laughed and fiddled with the wrapper. 'I always thought chocolate was better when shared. Want some?' He broke the nutty bar in half and handed the portion to her.

She took the chocolate and bit into it. 'So generous of you, thank you,' she said between mouthfuls.

He watched her devour the sweet in a millisecond. 'You're welcome. One chocolate addict to another; you would do the same.'

Bella walked towards the door. 'Assumptions like that can lead to misunderstandings.' She threw him a

wink before flitting through the door and leading him outside and to the house.

'So, you wouldn't share a chocolate bar with me? I had you all wrong,' he said.

She could hear the humour in his voice behind her.

She paused at the doorway and faced him. 'How could you have me in any which way, Mr Adams? You have only just met me,' she murmured before disappearing into the back door.

Merging through the crowd, Ace instilled himself near Warren and the group of men who had come searching for him. He peered towards the open doors of the ambulance where he noticed a body on the stretcher completely obscured with a white sheet. *Poor Terry. He didn't make it*, he thought, concealing the smirk that threatened to give him away. The sound of more sirens pierced through the hustle of noise as a police vehicle pulled into the dusty lot.

Ace watched while the police officers ventured into the crowd and began their investigation into the fatal snake attack. The hairs on his ears pricked as he honed into their conversation with Warren while he lurked behind them.

Warren's faded eyes crimped with worry. 'I pulled my daughter away just in time. It could've been her laying in that ambulance,' he anguished.

The policeman paused between jotted pen marks to look at Warren. 'Your daughter saw this snake up close?'

Warren nodded. 'Yeah, mate. She was under the bleachers with it; she was very lucky,' he said.

The policeman asked to speak with the girl. Ace casually meandered behind them as Warren and a few other men led the man to a bench along the side of the arena where his daughter sat curled in her mother's lap. The officer crouched onto his knees and introduced himself to the girl. His voice was gentle as he attempted to coax her into telling him her story.

She sat up in the folds of her mother's embrace while she listened to the policeman. Red-rimmed eyes watched him with fright when she was asked to recall the snake's description. Her long dark hair almost concealed her tiny face as she shook her head. 'He might come back for me if I tell. He wanted to hurt me. He told me that,' her voice trembled.

The policeman reached for the girl's hand and gave her a reassuring squeeze. 'He won't hurt you, Skye. Your daddy won't let him. Your mummy won't let him, and I won't let him,' he assured her.

'Skye, what do you mean, he told you?' Warren came to sit next to his daughter.

Her eyes filled with tears and toppled down her cheeks as she gazed around at the surrounding crowd. 'He was mean. I offered him my last musk stick and he threw it in the dirt. He told me he was going to hurt me. He talked, daddy,' she cried.

'Skye, what did the snake look like?' the policeman asked.

She looked at them one by one before her gaze fell on Ace in the background of the small mob around her. She froze suddenly, and raised a quivering hand through the air to point at him.

'Him,' her small voice caught in her throat. 'The snake looked like him, daddy.'

All heads turned to peer at Ace.

A grin irked across his face. 'Hello! Hi there,' he waved.

Warren leaned over to plant a kiss on his daughter's forehead and whispered in his wife's ear. He looked at the officer still on bent knees before them. 'She's in shock; can we finish this tomorrow?' he said.

The policeman rose to his feet. 'Sure,' he said, then ambled back to his partner who was raising his own questions among the onlookers.

With the crowd dispersing, Warren approached Ace. 'I'm sorry about that, she's only five years old,' he said glumly.

Ace forced a smile. 'It's okay. I'm used to it, everyone

says that,' he joked.

Warren extended a palm and introduced himself with a heavy sigh. 'I haven't seen you around here, passing by?'

'Just biding time, picking up work here and there,' he shrugged.

When he realised Ace was working at a nearby farm, Warren invited him to his own farm for dinner the following evening to discuss upcoming harvesting and machinery work he needed help with. 'It's the least I can do after my daughter's wild accusations,' he muttered.

Ace accepted the invitation without hesitation, his interest spiked with the pointed finger of Warren's daughter. *How could she know?*

'Say, are you and the fellas going to hunt that snake down?' he said as Warren turned to leave for his family.

The wiry wisps of his goatee bounced on his chin as he nodded. 'Sure am. You interested in gaming, son?'

His eyes sparkled. 'Oh, there is nothing I love more than a good hunt,' he said with relish.

Warren nodded with a grunt before heading to collect his wife and daughter to take them home.

Ace watched the thin man walk away. He was looking forward to this little episode mingling with the enemies that sought to kill him. It was all he could do to keep from chortling out loud.

'I knew it was you, snake-man.'

A voice from behind shattered the merriment that coursed through his bones. He turned to find the silhouette of the wild-haired witch he had met earlier.

His eyes narrowed. 'Are you following me, witch?'

She stepped closer. Pudgy ringed fingers dug into her cleavage as she fished out the stone emblem she sought. She held it up for him to see under the tarnished light of the night. He gazed at it with disinterest until he recognised the carved figure coiled within the green stone.

'Who are you?' he demanded.

Skin white as new fallen snow creased into a wide grin. 'I told you, I'm Madison,' she said, cocking her to the side as she let the emblem fall between her breasts. 'We are the same – you and me. I am a snake-queen, and you were sent here for me. Why don't you start by telling me your name?'

He glared at her, then trailed his eyes to the carved stone that dangled over her flannelette shirt. 'Where did you get that?' he scowled.

'From Apepsis. He is my serpent god. Yours too, no?' she said, her charcoal lined eyes curved into a slither with her smile.

Ace shrugged and watched her cautiously. 'My name is Ace,' he said.

She threw her frizzy head back and laughed. 'Of course it is! Ace – master of games – perfect. You are just perfect,' She studied him appreciatively. 'Come on, I have lots to show and tell, and I have food and wine. You must be ravenous after the taste of blood on your fangs.'

'Yeah,' Ace admitted.

'Follow me, Ace of games,' she teased, reaching for his hand to pull him into the dreary shadows of the bush.

Her fingers felt like the icy shards of a glacier and he briskly snatched his hand from hers. He continued to follow her deeper into the overgrowth. He was unsure if she could be trusted, but as he fell into step behind her, the hissing whispers of the black serpent beckoned him on. He had no choice but to follow her – his master called.

Chapter Four

July 24, 1998

Dear Journal,

How quickly things manifest when we totally surrender ourselves to the assumption of our desires. I am fast learning that action is far better taken after I have allowed my consciousness to expand enough to identify with my aspirations. For example, since I was a girl I imagined a life of a successful artist _ one that could generate enough income from her art alone. One that would be celebrated over the world for her creations. When I finally let go and yielded to my dream by identifying and resonating with it, I was able to believe my desire would find expression through me. That belief, that faith, is everything and all that we need to create our dreams.

Sounds simple, huh? If it's that easy, then why are the vast of us miserable in the lives we live? I cannot answer that; however, I suspect that it may have something to do with the limitations we impose upon ourselves. It seems that we have forgotten our divine roots, and our lives become determined by what we observe rather than resonating with our true essence.

But what if we are not sure what we want? What if we deny ourselves the very thing we want? What if we are torn between the past and the present and both are happening simultaneously?

It's funny how some memories are as clear as a static photograph in your mind ... so what is time anyhow but an earthly-bound concoction.

Some days I'm down by the willow tree enfolded in the arms of love. Most days this subject becomes harder and I am torn between the past and the now. Then what I really want becomes so jumbled it eludes me.

Millie xo

Millie watched the American journalist jot down notes in the notepad she balanced on her lap. They were midway through the interview for *New World Art* magazine. Slicked back mousy hair did not budge an inch with the fall of her head as the journalist peered intently into her papers. Nor did the locks shift when she lifted her head to gaze back at Millie.

A smile briefly appeared on thin lips. 'Are you aware two of your pieces were recently purchased for President Bill Clinton and American diplomat Richard Holbrooke?' she said.

Millie's eyes widened as she glanced towards Damon sitting beside her. 'Uh, no. I was not aware ... are you certain?' she gasped.

Damon shrugged as a wide grin spread across his face. 'Miss Grey, how did you come to hear this information? We know nothing of this.'

Millie recognised the excitement in the pitch of his voice.

'To answer both of your questions, I have reliable sources in Washington DC, and even more reliable sources throughout the American art world. I am quite certain of this new development,' she said.

A smile began to float over Millie's lips as the

information absorbed into her consciousness. She recalled the words of Samantha when she explained her
gift to charge each of her paintings with divine energy. *It
is your destiny to help shift the collective consciousness of
the world,* she had explained at the time. Now, she is beginning to see how the universe is conspiring to spread
her divine-infused creations to people within power.

'Wow,' she whispered.

The journalist glared at her through horn-rimmed
spectacles. 'Can you elaborate, please?' she enunciat-
ed, as if speaking to a young child. 'I mean, that is quite
impressive for a relatively unknown Australian artist,
wouldn't you say?'

Millie laughed. 'Yes, I would say, indeed. I am delighted,' she said, grinning at Damon. 'Of course, this is
the result of the relentless efforts of my marketing team.'

'I see,' Miss Grey murmured before wildly scribbling
in her notepad.

She pursued more questions about Damon's involvement and their relationship, and Millie's aspirations
for the future. After more furious writing, she paused to
study Millie.

'I took the liberty of researching your background,
Millie. I discovered your family's involvement in an attempted murder incident back in December, last year,'
she said, studying Millie for her reaction.

Millie felt the colour drain from her face and

thought her heart might stop in her chest. She squirmed a little in her chair and shot Damon a nervous glance. *This wasn't supposed to be part of the interview, surely?*

Damon protectively clasped his hand over hers.

'Miss Grey, we are here to talk about Millie's paintings, not her private life,' he said sternly.

The journalist glared at Damon. 'Mr Richards, the people that buy and read our magazine are just as interested in their favourite artists' lives as they are in their art work. Quite frankly, a controversial background such as Millie's can only enhance her attraction to her buyers, trust me,' she said.

With perfectly etched brows almost meeting her hairline, she turned her attention back to Millie. 'I made a few calls – one to The Rosebud Retreat where they said incident took place,' she said, glancing down at the notes in her lap. 'Although no arrests or charges were made, some people believe your brother, Ace, was responsible for the attack on your mother …' her voice trailed.

Millie cleared her throat and looked at Damon. An image of shock froze across his features – he knew nothing of that incident back in December the year before. Her eyes flashed when she turned back to the journalist. 'Miss Grey, you are very thorough, no doubt about that. However sometimes, being thorough does not equate to being correct. Like you said, no charges were made and my brother had absolutely nothing to do with the attack on my mother. In fact, nobody knows who assaulted her that night – not even my mother,' she asserted.

The journalist slowly nodded her head before returning to her notes.

'So how is your mother doing now?' she asked, without looking up from her papers.

'My mother is doing great now.'

The pen in her hand paused as she glanced at Millie. 'And your brother?' she said.

Millie could barely conceal the scowl in her voice. 'My brother is great too.' She glanced towards the clock on the wall behind the woman. 'Are we done here? I've someplace else to be.'

A smile caught the edge of the journalist's lips. 'Yes, we are done. Thank you so much for your time, Millie. Would you mind if I took a look at your paintings on display?' she said, gesturing around the gallery.

Millie rose to her feet. 'Be my guest. Mrs Bartlett will show you out when you are done.' She took the hand Miss Grey offered and shook it briefly.

Millie picked up her coat and made for the back door of the gallery. The door slammed closed behind her, causing her to jump at the sudden noise. She leaned against the cold brick wall between the gallery and her studio, filling her lungs with the crisp winter air. She had been caught off guard. She had not expected the journalist to bring up the day her brother had murdered

their mother.

'Shit!' she cursed out loud. 'Shit, shit shit!'

'Shit, alright.' The door swung on its hinges to reveal Damon. 'Millie, what on earth was that all about?'

'Nothing,' she muttered.

Damon's face screwed up. 'Nothing? That is your explanation?' he said.

She turned her back to him and walked down the narrow alley towards her studio. She reached for the door handle and pulled the door ajar, only to find Damon's towering figure behind her wedging the door shut again.

Her eyes blazed at him. 'Damon! Move out of the way,' she demanded.

'Nope,' he said.

She pulled on the handle with all her strength. When she realised the door would not budge an inch with even her strongest effort, she stamped her feet like a little child and grumbled beneath her breath.

Damon chuckled at her outburst. 'Millie, why won't you talk to me?' he said softly.

The furrow in her brows deepened. 'Open the door, Damon.'

He moved aside and allowed her to open the door. He followed her inside the studio, closing the door behind him. When he spun around to face her, she noticed the intensity of his expression.

'You don't need to know everything, Damon,' she

said, leaning against a bench that ran the length of the studio.

'Not everything. Just everything about you,' he said.

'Not everything about me is your business,' she snapped.

'If I'm going to market and promote your work, I need to be prepared for journalists bringing up pivotal snippets of your past. I felt clueless back there!' he said, flinging his arms up in front of him.

He paused and regarded her. 'You know what? Forget that, Millie. I'm tired of you treating me like some acquaintance you hardly know. For the last six months, you've managed to keep me at arm's length – a business partner. Look around you, Millie, I'm still here! Me. Me. Remember me? Because I sure as hell remember you. I'm not going anywhere, and I have a feeling you don't want me to go anywhere. So, I'm asking you, how do you really want me in your life?' The last of his words brushed across her ears in a heated whisper.

When she looked up, she felt all the barriers she had erected since his arrival back into her life strip away like a plaster tearing from a wound. She became aware of her heart thumping wildly as butterflies awakened and churned among the feelings she had fought hard to repress for six long months. Her breath quickened as they began to take hold and flourish through her without permission.

'Damon … I just don't know how to pick up the pieces, the past …' She lowered her eyes, searching the paint-splattered floor for answers. 'So many nights I closed my eyes and spoke to you in a thousand different ways. My soul, my heart bared all until there was no more to reveal. I had to move on, for Arella, for me …'

He moved closer still. 'The past has no place in the present, Millie. You of all people know this,' he murmured and cupped his hand beneath her chin, bringing his lips to mesh against hers.

For one a sweet moment, she was back under the willow tree. Instinctively, her lips parted and released the passion that lay dormant beneath the surface for so long. They had only made love that one day years ago, but her body had not forgotten an inch of his. She responded with a yearning that took her by surprise as she kissed him back with the full force of her desire.

Hands fumbled to touch and feel the warmth of skin. Tongues once reacquainted, were unable to part, pushed and probed together in a delicious reunion of lust. So engrossed and captivated were they in the moment, they failed to hear the swing of the door as it opened.

Craig stood tall in the doorway to the studio. His lanky figure was transfixed and rooted to the floor while his mouth gaped at the scene before him. He cleared his throat with a loud rumble.

Millie caught his image in the corner of her eye. She

jerked away from Damon abruptly, wiping at her moist lips before clutching a handful of dark hair.

'Craig. I'm sorry … I didn't mean for that to happen,' she said. Fingers began to twirl furiously.

Eyes flooded with agony peered at her in silence.

Damon spun around and leaned against the bench next to her. A look of triumph crossed his face when he noticed Craig's expression.

'Craig,' he nodded curtly, a little too much smug infecting his voice.

Craig ignored him and continued to search Millie's face. 'So, you've made a choice then?' his voice hollow.

Millie shook her head and stepped towards him. She hadn't meant for this to happen. *It can't go down this way! How could I let it go this far?*

'No! Craig, it just happened. I wasn't thinking … I'm sorry,' she pleaded for the understanding she knew she didn't deserve.

Craig nodded and held up a hand to stop her in her tracks. 'I understand, Millie,' he said. He dragged his eyes from hers and turned away. The long black tails of his trench coat lapped the corner of the door before he disappeared down the alley way.

Silence hung in the room as Millie digested the events that had just occurred. She slowly turned and looked at Damon; her expression bore the heart that shattered beneath her breast.

He watched her closely. 'You didn't mean for that to happen, Millie?' he said.

She shrugged in defeat. 'I don't. I don't anything right now.' She slumped into a chair beside the bench.

'Well I do. The bond between you and I was strong enough to bring us together again – despite your father's efforts at keeping us apart when I tried contacting you over and over. Our bond will endure anything, Millie,' he said.

He walked to her and gently smoothed back her hair.

She gave him a small smile. 'I need some time to think, Damon. Would you mind?' she said.

'Sure,' he said, leaning to brush his lips against her forehead. Then he left her alone in the studio to ponder her thoughts.

'The energy will always go where it's directed,' she muttered to herself as she watched the door swing closed.

She had been under that willow tree again and again in her thoughts. She always knew it would come to pass again.

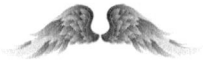

Bella cupped her hands over her mother's. She squeezed gently and looked at their entwining fingers for a moment. Never could she remember her mother's hands appearing so fragile before this day. Gone were the sure strong hands that would scoop her up and hold her close as a child when she awakened with nightmares. Lost were firm fingers that would run through her hair as her mother tied it back for school.

She swallowed the tears that blinded her eyes as her gaze drifted to her mother's sleeping face. They had not long arrived home from the doctor's rooms where they had received her mother's recent test results following her bout of radiation therapy.

She had almost fainted in those rooms. The words that the doctor uttered struck her like a bloody sword when he revealed her mother's fate. His compassionate horn-rimmed eyes had studied them silently before he spoke.

'I'm sorry, Rose, Annabella,' he uttered before visibly inhaling. 'The cancer has not responded as we had hoped. In fact, the tumour has worsened. It has spread into other parts of the body and has evolved into what we call, metastatic cancer. Unfortunately, metastatic stomach cancer is not considered to be curable.'

He continued to speak yet his words drowned in Bella's ears. It was then that her world began to spin. Her eyes were open, she was sure, yet she could see nothing – not the balding doctor with the speckled brown eyes that bore news of the inevitable death of another parent, nor her mother who sat beside her as silent as the dead of night.

'It's important at this stage that we keep you as comfortable as possible.'

'I am referring you to book a room in Calvary Hospital … 24-hour, around the clock care …'

The words jumbled around her mind and danced in a spin until she could string them together again.

'No!' she blurted loudly, 'She's not going to Calvary. People don't leave that hospital. No-one gets better there. No-one!' She shook her head and peered at her mother.

Rose smiled with resignation at her daughter.

'Mum? Tell him you're not going there,' she pleaded.

Her mother placed her hand over Bella's. Her hand was as cold as a sheet of ice, despite the warmth in the doctor's room.

'It's going to be okay, pumpkin. Calvary sounds just like the place I need right now. Better for me there,' she said.

Bella was unable to choke back the tears. 'But mum,' she cried.

Rose rubbed her daughter's hands. 'Now, now Bella,' she crooned, 'we'll discuss this at home later.'

The warmth of her mother's voice sliced through the chill that anguished Bella's heart, and she agreed to talk more about Calvary when they arrived home. Memories of the life-filled joyful woman who raised her filled her senses as she regarded the weakened woman before her. Thinning white hair clumped in sparse strings over an age-spotted scalp that crowned the sunken pasty skin of her face. Each shallow breath came short and barely noticeable under the flaccid movement of her chest.

Bella pressed the palm of her hand over her chest to make sure she was still breathing. She sighed heavily and rose to place a kiss on her mother's forehead before leaving her to sleep. They would talk more when she regained her strength. The morning's outing had depleted her energy entirely.

She went to the kitchen and rummaged through a cupboard until her hands found what she sought. Shaky fingers tore at the foiled chocolate wrapper, and once opened, she stuffed the sweet concoction into her mouth. As she swallowed the caramel infused chocolate bar, a fleeting feeling of comfort waved through her. *I need more!* she thought, kicking into action in search of more chocolate.

Her mission came to a sudden halt when the sound of the doorbell chimed through the quiet house. She froze, lifting her head to curiously eye the box above her that housed the chiming sound, as if it might reveal her visitor.

It sounded again and she flew down the narrow hallway to answer the door before it disturbed her mother. She was surprised to see Craig when she drew the door open. He stood tall and smiling with a leather satchel bag strapped over his chest and large box next to his feet. Bella smiled through darkly lashed eyes. Brushing a lock of her shoulder-length hair from her face, she clutched at the ends in a twist.

'Mr Adams, I wasn't expecting you today,' she said, trailing her gaze to the rectangular box next to him.

'Craig,' he corrected, 'and I know, I have some papers for you and your mother to sign. I was driving past and saw your car in the drive. I hope you don't mind.' He gestured towards the large box. 'Besides, I bring gifts.'

'That's okay, come in,' she smiled.

She led him to the back of the house and into the kitchen. 'Tea?' she asked over her shoulder.

Craig dropped the box to the floor before loosening the belt of his trench coat. 'That would be lovely,' he said.

Silently focusing on her tea-making task, the slender curve of her shoulders slumped as she was lost in the hot swirling liquid as she stirred it.

He watched her thoughtfully. 'Hard day?' he asked as she brought the tea to the table where he had some papers splayed out for her to look at.

She sighed. 'Yeah. They want to admit my mum to Calvary,' she said.

Craig nodded. 'I'm so sorry, Bella,' he sympathised.

She forced a short smile, noticing the compassion in his eyes, and the empathy in his voice. It was all she could do to not break down again. Instead, she cleared her throat and swallowed hard. 'So, what's that?' she said, pointing to the box.

Craig chuckled lightly. 'Open and see,' he said.

Hesitantly, she leaned to unfold the cardboard flaps, and gasped when she caught sight of a new heater. 'Craig, I can't accept this,' she said, shaking her head.

'Yes you can, Bella. You see, I bought this a few months back when I thought my life was on track,' he sighed. 'Things have changed and I have no use for it now; my apartment is small and I already have heating. I was going to give it to charity, but then ... last week when I was here ...'

He shrugged and regarded the heater with the eyes of a lost puppy dog. Bella watched him closely. This man she hardly knew had somehow crept in and moved her soul in ways she had not ever known, and it puzzled her. For the first time since he had arrived, she really looked at him. Her heart sank as she recognised the weary expression that etched his features, revealing his own inner turmoil.

He tore his eyes from the boxed heater between them. 'Please accept it, Bella,' he said.

Her head bowed as she lowered her eyes. As her stare found the knot of her twisting fingers, she became aware of the burn that slowly crept up and flushed through her cheeks. She gave a quick nod and avoided his eyes.

Craig watched her while the silence between them stretched to an uncomfortable lull. They were both startled when the doorbell chime echoed through the soundless kitchen. Bella excused herself with an air of relief wafting over her as she made a dash for the front door.

'Hi Bella-rella, how did it go this morning? How is she?' Emma stood in the doorway, her dark eyes swimming with concern while she grasped at a cluster of shopping bags.

'Hi Em. She's resting, come in,' Bella took some bags from her friend and led her towards the kitchen.

Emma waffled on while following her. 'I have chocolates, salt and vinegar chips, popcorn and for old-time's sake – *Pretty Woman*,' she chirped.

'Gotta love *Pretty Woman*,' Bella mumbled.

'Well, yeah. Oh, and I have a big bottle of Coke and …' Emma stopped short when she rounded the doorway and caught sight of Craig sitting in the kitchen.

'Oh, hello.' Emma's surprise immediately overturned into a smooth purr. Short fingers flew up to straighten her mousy brown hair, and ample breasts strained against the knit blouse she wore as she unravelled her slumping frame. Crooked teeth gleamed bright. 'And who might you be?'

Craig smiled and gathered his satchel bag. 'Craig Adams. Bella's real estate agent.' He offered his hand.

She took his hand and pumped eagerly. 'Emma Hudson. Nice to meet you.' She shot Bella a not-so-conspicuous look.

Craig turned to Bella as he pulled on his coat. 'I'll leave the sale contracts for you to go over. Drop them into the office whenever you're going by; no rush,' he remarked with a tired smile.

'Sure.'

He pulled something from his satchel bag before scooping it up and flinging it over his shoulder. 'Oh, I wanted to give you this.' He pushed a business card into her hand.

She glimpsed towards the card as she took it from him. 'Holly's art studio?' Her eyes widened.

Craig pushed a lingering curl from his brow. 'Yeah. I know Holly, and I know she would love your sculptures. Give her a call,' he said casually, turning to Emma to bid his goodbyes.

Bella watched his exit with a mix of uncertainty and reprieve. 'Bye Craig. And thanks,' she mumbled, closing the door behind him.

She exhaled and leaned against the wooden frame, gazing at the card and turning it over and over with steeple fingers. She closed her eyes to steady the slight upbeat of her heart. *Where did that come from?* she thought, surprised by her racing pulse.

'Bella!' Emma's soft call trailed down the quiet hall of the house.

Bella inched off the door. 'Coming,' she replied, grateful for the distraction of her friend.

Chapter Five

July 31, 1998

Dear Journal,

It has been a week since I have seen Craig. A week since he discovered a stolen kiss. And while I feel terrible for the hurt I know I have caused him, I cannot help but envision that moment with the stirring of sweet tinges.

Does that make me a bad person? It's just, it has been so long since I have known Damon's intimate touch upon my skin ... and the warmth of his kiss against my own _ not only was it exquisite to feel him again, it also felt like coming home.

Damon evokes the deepest feelings of physical and spiritual hunger within me; I don't know how to deny it much longer.

When I asked Samantha for her advice, she told me only that love is the recognition of our true being, and the cornerstone in the desire for human fusion — she may be my guiding angel yet at times her advice baffles me!

I do not want to see Craig feeling any which way but happy. I wish I could ease his turmoil, yet I know now that I am not the one for him.

Last night my brother impressed himself upon my dream world. His essence draws closer, stronger as he ponders his revenge.

I believe that there is only one force in all the universe which creates according to what we conceive and allow — the right use of this power will create a blessing, while the wrong use will create harm. It works for evil as much as for love. And it's evil that grips the heart of my brother.

Millie xo

The glint of his eyes deepened and frolicked against the gentle lick of flames as Ace lost himself to the devouring seduction of the fire. He leaned forward and clenched his hands high above his head in a lazy stretch. The rippling contours of his muscular body gleamed and shadowed naked under the incandescent glow of the room. A drowsy smile appeared as he marvelled at the change in his life since he had met Madison.

He had followed her to this humble cottage only two weeks earlier, yet he felt as if he had known her a lifetime. He fell back against the soft pile of a woollen rug as the last two weeks drifted through his thoughts.

'Where are you taking me?' he demanded with a sudden halt.

They had been trekking through the damp foliage for some twenty minutes, and as each step grew soggier beneath his feet, so too had his impatience.

Madison stopped to regard him. 'I told you, I'm taking you to my home. It's not far now, C'mon,' she insisted, with a shake of her blazing curls.

Ace scowled. *I should have just killed her*, he seethed.

A ring-decorated hand reached out and grasped at his fingers. 'C'mon, Ace of games. I won't hurt you,' she taunted.

He snatched his hand from hers with a grunt, then stepped closer to her. 'Believe me, I am not afraid of you. And don't fucking touch me,' he snarled. White teeth glistened with the streaks of moonlight falling through the trees.

She threw a dirty glance over her shoulder and shrugged. 'Suit yourself. You'll be singing a different tune soon enough,' she chimed.

Ace scowled again and followed her in silence. His suspicion was unable to overcome the compelling urge to follow her. This unusual occurrence only served to annoy him even more. *Apepsis.* The name twisted through his mind with the painful uncoiling of a long-kept sordid secret. The thought of knowing the serpent master's name was enough to evoke a titillating sensation through him. He knew he had to find out more.

The dense shrub eventually gave way to a clearing, and a small stone cottage came into view. He filled his lungs with the whiff of smoke as it curled from the chimney and into the cold night. He inhaled deeply. He loved the smell of burning wood. And there was something else. He drew another breath and became aware of his empty stomach. Irish stew.

'This is where you live?' he said, following her up the porch steps.

Much like a child, she skipped up the stairs and flung the door open. 'Yep, for now,' she grinned. 'Hungry?'

Ace nodded and followed her inside. He sat by the fire while she banged pots and pans together in the kitchen before emerging with a generous bowl of Irish lamb stew and a glass of red wine.

'Hope you like red wine,' she stammered.

Suddenly appearing vulnerable, she placed the bowl and burgundy filled glass on the coffee table before him.

He watched her, drinking in her short, buxom image now that his view was not tainted by the dark. His eyes drifted to the emblem around her neck. Instinctively, her fingers found the emblem and she stroked it lovingly as she beamed towards him.

His eyes met hers with the frost of ice. 'Talk,' he commanded.

He ravenously picked up the steaming bowl of stew, and settled back to hear what had brought him all the way to this cottage.

Madison perched on the sofa opposite him. 'Apepsis is the serpent god. The personification of evil. Since the beginning of time, Apepsis has sought to reign power over this world, and since the beginning of time, the Ascended Angels have strived to stop him. Each utilise humans in their will to triumph. Through incarnations to planting seeds to metamorphism, humans provide their only means to physicality,' she said.

Ace paused between mouthfuls and frowned. 'Why does Apepsis want power over this world,' he said.

'Apepsis has been shunned from all other realms. The Ascended Angels, the Cherubs, and the gods inhabit all others. Earth was assigned for the freewill of humans to make their own paths and lessons that would eventually lead them back towards the light. Apepsis lives in between. Earth is his last resort to claim for himself as humans can make for easy manipulation in his desire to populate the earth with his will.'

Ace nodded. 'Okay. Sounds pretty heavy.' He took a swig of wine. 'Why does he come to me?'

Ruby coloured lips spread wide. 'Because you have allowed him. You have more power than anyone I have heard to possess. I mean, I had heard of Apepsis using the powers of shape-shifting upon humans, but you are the first I have known,' she said.

For the first time Ace noticed the smattering of freckles that littered her face. *Cute freckles.*

She lowered her head and gazed at him through thick lashes. 'That makes you kinda special,' she said coyly.

'And those freckles make you kinda dishy,' he remarked.

He took another sip of the wine and sprawled back in the sofa with a smoky grin.

She threw him a dazzling smile and dropped to her knees. 'Apepsis promises riches and power to his loyal followers,' she said huskily as she began a slow crawl towards him. 'I can help you, Ace of games.'

He watched her every move through seductive

eyes, and when she reached him, he squirmed slightly against the bulge that pressed against the confines of the tight jeans he had stolen. The only sound in the room came from the irregular spit and crackles of the fire. She unbuttoned her shirt and removed her lacy black bra.

'Together, there are no limits. Just tell me where we start. I am yours,' she murmured.

His lips parted slightly to reveal the sweep of his tongue as his eyes rested on the strawberry coloured nipples that swelled in offering before him. Her pale skin glowed vividly in the light of the fire and her tizzy hair blazed over darkly provocative eyes, giving her a lustrous appearance.

A plump hand reached for the strain of his groin, and with one swift movement he was unzipped and released. He clutched handfuls of frizzy red tresses while throbbing against the firm grip of her fingers, pulsating under the hot flickers of her tongue, and palpitating within the pleasurable suckling of her mouth. His grasp on her tightened and he restrained her head firmly as he reached his peak and released a throaty groan along with an arousing climax.

He allowed his body to relax, and slumped back into the sofa again with a gratifying smirk.

He looked around the cottage for a moment. His interest perked when he noticed some shelves laden with jars of various sizes full of herbs, moss and liquid-like substances. String, bone needles, poppets and crooked wands were laid out in an orderly fashion next to an iron cauldron.

He traced his eyes back down to her, still on her knees before him. 'First we start with some fun. We shall eat with Warren Glassop and his family tomorrow night.' His eyes darkened with the shadow of his sneer. 'Then we will travel to Sydney and pay a visit to my dear sister.'

Her smile danced with the melody of the flames that warmed the room. She rose to her feet and slipped out of her jeans. She kicked them away and straddled him. 'So, tell me about your dear sister,' she said.

Her voice was like honey.

Ace and Madison were greeted with an onslaught of barking dogs when the Harley Davidson pulled up outside the Glassop homestead the next evening. Ace wedged down the kick stand with his boot and dismounted the bike. He turned and helped Madison's short figure disembark, groping a big hand down her V-neck sweater as he did so. He pulled her close, holding her from behind while pressing himself rigidly against her soft, plump body. It had been so long since he had held a woman. Never had a woman provoked more than just flitting lust within him. *At last, a woman who may hold my interest!* he thought, nuzzling promises against her skin with his lips.

Madison moulded into his towering body like jelly suctioning against its cup. She grinded her fleshy skirted bottom into his groin and lifted her chin back towards him. 'Steady cowboy, dessert will come later,' she teased.

The dogs scurried and growled near their feet.

Ace regarded them with amusement. He leaned towards them, his eyes flashed and his head cocked to one side. He centred himself, and in one deliberate action he opened his mouth wide. White pointed fangs gleamed and twisted, exposing themselves in a vicious snarl. The dogs instantly backed off as they curled in their tails and ran away in yelping whimpers.

Ace clasped Madison's hand while they laughed and made for the homestead. 'This is going to be fun,' Ace said, squeezing her hand lightly.

Warren answered their knocking with a watery smile. His smile waned when he saw Madison standing next to Ace.

Ace took Warren's bony hand in a shake. 'This is Madison. I hope you don't mind that I brought along a companion,' he beamed.

Warren gave Madison a curt nod. 'I know who she is …' His voice trailed and his thin lips pursed beneath his goatee.

'Oh?' Madison's eyes narrowed, 'I'm sorry; have we met before?'

Warren shook his head. 'I don't think so. But everyone in town knows the likes of you; you're the witch,' he said, pointing an accusing finger towards her.

Ace and Madison exchanged an amused look.

'Don't be silly old mate,' Ace laughed. 'Small towns breed big bullshit.' He clasped an arm around Warren and began to lead him into the house.

Warren introduced them to his wife, Sheila. She regarded them suspiciously, yet Ace could not fault her accommodating nature towards her guests. She quietly set about seating Skye close to Warren before serving them a roast dinner, bread and whiskey, barely glancing their way throughout the whole process.

'I asked around town. I heard-tell you were good at working the land. Good with machinery too,' Warren said while chewing a mouthful of meaty gravy.

Ace nodded. 'Yeah. You needing a hand with those pineapple crops?'

'Yep. Can you start this week? I have a bed over the barn, and all meals included,' Warren said.

'Oh, he won't be needing a bed,' Madison interjected. She threw Ace an alluring grin. 'He'll stay with me.'

Ace returned her grin with a wink. 'Ahh … I can give you a hand here and there, but I'll be leaving for a while soon. Family business in Sydney.'

Warren took a generous sip of his whiskey. His deep-set watery eyes strained to focus against the streaks of blood that webbed across them. 'Rightio, then,' he nodded grimly. He gestured towards the table. 'Let me help Sheila in the kitchen, then we'll talk about hunting down this snake tomorrow.'

Suddenly Sheila's voice penetrated through the room like a choir hymn. 'The light shines in the darkness, and the darkness has not overcome it: John 1:5,' she chanted.

All eyes settled on her.

'Sheila?' Warren exclaimed. His scrawny face scrunched into a frown. 'What are you going on about, woman?'

She directed her hazel gaze at Ace. 'Turn from evil and do good, seek peace and pursue it. I beg you. It's not too late for you.' Her voice was insistent.

Ace held her stare and cautiously smiled. For a moment his blackened heart saw a glimmer of light and leaped for joy. *Could she be right?*

Warren thumped a balled fist against the table. 'Enough, Sheila! You're spooking our guests.' He rose to his feet. 'Let's clean up.'

Sheila silently groped for the empty plates and cutlery but would not look at Ace and Madison. When they reached the kitchen, Ace heard Warren's low grumbles through the thin walls.

Madison squeezed Ace's hand. 'Spooky! Be right back,' she whispered in his ear, before leaving the room to offer help in the kitchen.

Finally Ace was left with Skye without her parents around. He turned to her with a smile, catching the visible shudder in her brown eyes.

'You've been very quiet, little miss. Cat got your tongue?' he grinned.

She shook her head, slinging her long brown hair over her shoulders.

'Hmmm … a dog maybe?'

Another shake, and her dark eyes grew as wide as a pottery wheel.

Ace leaned towards her. His eyes peered up at the ceiling for a moment as if in deep thought. 'I know,' he exclaimed with mischief twinkling over his face. He looked back to her. 'It must be a snake then! A snake has caught your little tongue.'

Skye gasped and jumped in her seat.

He laughed. 'Your tongue was working fine last night when you told everyone I was the snake,' he said.

In a courageous move, she poked her tongue out at him before pursing her lips tight.

Ace's face softened as he watched her. Her long dark hair and big eyes reminded him of Arella. He missed his little niece more than he cared to admit.

'Did you know the tongue is the fastest healing part

of the body?' he said.

Skye shook her head again, only this time her eyes lit up with curiosity. 'Is your tongue forked?' she ventured quietly.

Ace chuckled. 'Well, let's see,' he said.

He protruded his tongue out towards her and watched in amusement as her eyes scoured over it thoroughly.

She grinned. Satisfied his tongue was like her own, she proceeded to poke her own tongue back out towards him.

They wriggled and curled them about in the air together before bursting into giggles. Shelia entered the room with an expression of disapproval, and both stiffened and looked at her like naughty little children. She pushed back an imaginary strand of her grey-streaked mousy hair that was pulled tightly into a bun and scurried over to her daughter.

Her lips clung together in a thin line. 'That's enough Skye, time for bed.' She pulled at her daughter's arm.

'Okay, mummy,' Skye answered and followed her mother from the room.

She paused and turned to Ace. 'Next time will you eat my candy?'

Ace grinned. 'Promise,' he said.

She smiled and skipped out of the room.

Sheila stopped at the door and looked at him. Her

eyes shadowed for a moment. 'Love will set you free. Love or suffer. Claim it or …,' she croaked and disappeared through the doorway, leaving him to contemplate her words.

The next morning Ace joined Warren and two other men in their quest for a large black snake. They met in the dusty carpark of the rodeo arena, and armed with rifles and axes, agreed to split up and scour the surrounding bush.

Ace trekked into the wild backwoods with Greggo, a short man sporting a long beard, an Aussie bush hat and a hefty gut.

'His track seems to stop here,' Greggo called out through the shrubbery. He was standing by a thick overthrown tree trunk.

Ace ventured closer. He regarded the man as he approached him, curbing the disgust that rose in his throat when he noticed the curls of wiry hair that protruded from his backside between his trousers and sweater.

'Fricking dirty trickster snake. Must be a smart one, that one,' Greggo said.

He turned his head with a throaty hurl and spat a thick green golly into the trees. 'I'm gonna rip his head off and cook him for dinner when I catch him,' he gloated.

A few drops of spittle clung to the ends of his beard, threatening to drop with each word he uttered.

Ace raised an eyebrow. 'Ha! I'd like to see that,' he muttered.

Greggo bent down to peer closer at the track. 'This just doesn't seem to make sense. Something else has gone on here.' He traced a grubby finger through the dirt.

Ace looked down at the squatting man, unable to disguise his grimace when he caught sight of the deep hairy crevice between his buttocks that his pants revealed.

He tore his eyes away. 'Where are the others?' He couldn't hear Warren and the other man. They must have been deep into the adjacent bush by now.

Greggo chuckled and hauled himself up. 'Why, you scared pretty boy?' he retorted.

Ace threw him an icy stare. 'I'm going this way,' He gestured over his shoulder.

The tubby man grunted a reply and lumbered away.

Ace delved deeper into the bush and stopped when he discovered a huge crevice in the trunk of a big gum tree. *Perfect!* He smiled and began to undress.

He folded his belongings and placed them carefully in the tree crevice before crawling within its damp cavity. He closed his eyes and began to breathe deeply. He felt all resistance drain from his body and welcomed the shift in his awareness as he began the transformation.

He beckoned the presence of Apepsis to consume him, and when the glint of white fangs became visible to him, he allowed himself to be totally engulfed until the union was complete.

Ace fixed his thoughts towards his curled figure below and savoured the agony as he entered the denseness of a physical body again; now with senses that were razor sharp and a mouth an armed deadly weapon.

A big black head extended from the crevice. Ace squinted against the light for a moment and inhaled deeply while tasting the air for the scent he desired. He grimaced in loathing when the slight stench of stale alcohol combined with days old grime filled his senses and ran rancid between his sensory glands. Shiny scales flexed under the involuntary writhing that permeated through him before he set off in a stealthy slither towards his quarry, his long thick body uncoiled with the grace of a perfect trail behind him.

Let's see whose head will be ripped off today, he mused as he stole silently near Greggo. He paused behind a thick bush and took solace among the long unruly blades of grass that carpeted the wooded floor of the forest.

He watched the short-bearded man as Greggo slumped his bulky body on a log and took out a pouch of tobacco. Blubbery fingers fumbled a tobacco filled paper between them, and he mumbled something inaudible under his breath. Bringing the unlit cigarette to his lips, he bit down to chew off the papery end between yellowed teeth before turning his beard to spit the thin soggy paper to the ground.

Ace moved soundlessly on a bed of dampened earth and moist fallen leaves, pausing only when the consistent muttering ceased.

'Snakey, snakey where are you?' Greggo sang. His eyes peered beneath the bush hat while he looked over the quiet bush. 'Ima gonna be the one to catch you.'

Involved in his sing-song, he missed the sudden commotion of the birds above as their chirps shrilled while they took refuge in flight. Greggo chuckled to himself and inhaled his fill of charring tobacco. It was then his mumbling crooning wavered and he cocked his head to one side in sudden alarm.

A deathly silence filled the woods. The small break of a twig echoed through the bush with an earth-shattering crack, and when Greggo turned to peer behind him, his widening eyes met with a cobalt shimmer.

Greggo jolted back in surprise. Reeling off the log and landing with a thud on a blanket of damp leaves, he scrambled for his rifle only a few feet away. Thickened fingers grappled desperately in the earth as he threw a glance upward to find his gaze swallowed by the sight of

white incisors seeping with droplets of venom.

The overweight man froze beneath the snake's steely presence as he poised over him threateningly. Ace's pearl blue eyes danced with amusement as he caught the petrified look in his quarry's eyes. He drew a quick breath and with the greatest of pleasure exhaled all his air over Greggo in a long warm hiss.

A squawking grunt escaped through Greggo's lips as he stumbled over onto his knees in an awkward attempt to get to his feet. It was at this moment that Ace lunged. The length of his five-inch fangs found the putrid skin of Greggo's neck and sank with the force of a deep strike as he manipulated his scaly sinuous body to entwine his prey. Ace constricted his thick coils, stopping only with the last of the gurgling sounds issued from Greggo's mouth and all his breath had been pushed out of him.

A hush befell the bush, an eerie silence that preceded the happening of death and touched the falling shadows of the trees. Not an animal could be heard, and as Ace contemplated using his pointed teeth to tear the head off the man that had threatened to take his own, a darkness emanated through a cluster of large tree trunks nearby.

Ace raised his head when he felt the presence overcome him, and as he peered into the inkiness between the trees, he instinctively bared hissing fangs with a dangerous flash of his eyes.

A low chortling sound rolled out from the darkness and yellow eyes became visible as if suspended in a blanket of black.

'Ace … come closer,' it beckoned.

Ace loosened his long coils and cautiously slinked closer to the beaming yellow eyes. He knew his visitor's name now, and he knew his essence intimately.

He paused where the darkness met the light in a line of vibrant contrast. 'Apepsis?' he said.

'I am Apepsis. We are pleased with your progress. More power awaits you, Ace,' Apepsis sneered. A sizzle echoed from the black. 'With each shift, you will become more powerful and your form will expand; destroy the last of the ascended bloodlines and victory will be ours.'

Ace peered into the shadows with confusion. 'Who are these bloodlines?' he asked.

A long drawn out hiss resounded from the gloom among the trunks and reverberated through Ace's ears.

He flinched.

Apepsis fell silent and Ace was unsure if he still lurked in the inky shadows. He studied the darkness in search of the yellow eyes. Suddenly they flashed before him like studded lights, so close it began to unnerve him.

'The feminine offspring of your family,' Apepsis whispered. 'You were already on the right path. Now go!'

The yellow eyes faded into the shadows and the darkness lifted with the roll of a heavy fog.

Ace became aware of Warren's thundering footsteps and the other snake hunter as they drew closer. He glanced back to Greggo, now laying flaccid upon the earth that soaked the steady stream of blood leaking from his throat.

A brief feeling of remorse seeped through him, and as he slithered away with the thrust of great speed behind him, a vision of his sister fogged his mind. *Millie-pie … my silly Millie-pie*, he thought.

He reached the cavity of the tree trunk where his clothes lay folded neatly and waiting. When he performed the ritual that would shift his body into its former shape, he lay cold and shivering in a curved ball of anguish. *How did I get this far …?* He sobbed into the heart of the tree that consumed his torment with an unconditional, accepting ear. The words of Sheila the night before crowded his mind under a golden-violet ray.

Madison sashayed into the room with a bath towel wrapped around her damp body. She handed Ace a steaming mug of freshly brewed coffee and threw an appreciative gaze over his nakedness, pausing when her dark eyes found his shaft laying flaccid and resting against his upper thigh. His skin glowed with the warmth of the fire under her stare. A lopsided grin marked his face as he watched the hunger in her eyes growing in unison with the hardening of his male member. He placed his mug aside and reached for the edge of the towel that swathed her. He tugged and in one swift movement her kneeling plump body was exposed. He noticed the heave of her chest as she gasped audibly and the gentle swell of her nipples as they became erect under his provocative gaze.

He reached out to catch the green stone emblem that nestled between the generous curves of her breasts and tugged again. She willingly leaned closer to him, and allowed another gasp to escape her lips when his other hand found the soft folds between her thighs. His eyes held hers firmly in a seductive game of wills as his stare dared her to lose all control.

'Come my witch. Come with me,' he murmured.

The alluring tone of his words was enough for her to reach her threshold. She moved the white flesh of her legs to encompass the length of him and moaned louder and louder with each penetrating thrust until the gush flowed from within her to the sweet melody of their lovemaking.

Afterwards they lay snuggled in an entwining cocoon of flushed skin and tingling moist delight. Frank Sinatra's *The Way You Look Tonight* filtered mildly through the room against the crackles of the fire. Ace smiled lazily and glanced down at the woman in his arms. He liked the way she felt so close to him. He blew a gentle breath of warm air into her ear.

'We leave in the morning,' he said huskily.

'To see your sister?' she inquired.

He nodded. His brows creased thoughtfully as a plan revealed itself in his mind's eye. 'Hmmm …. Or rather we will make her comes to us. So much quieter here than in Sydney,' he said.

Madison smirked. 'Nobody around to hear her screams,' she cooed.

'Exactly,' Ace chuckled. His expression darkened. 'Never trust a sleeping snake – we can see right through our eyelids.'

He reached for her waist playfully and gave her a little tickle. She squirmed under his light poking fingers and laughed.

'Have you ever thought about why you're so ticklish?' he murmured.

Her eyes narrowed with her smile. 'No,' she said with a shake of her frizzy red head.

His expression grew serious. 'Your tickle sensation is your body's reflex warning you to something that may potentially harm you,' he said.

His voice was almost a hiss.

Chapter Six

August 15, 1998

Dear Journal,

There is nothing that comes into physical form that is not first perfected in the higher planes of consciousness – these are the words of my angel and for my use to ponder this week. When my thoughts shift to Craig and Damon, I can see how this makes sense. For my thoughts and desires have longed for Damon ever since he reappeared in my life. No more has transpired between us intimately since that afternoon Craig saw us kissing. I cannot pursue a relationship with Damon until Craig will talk with me ... until I can find the right time for truth and tell Damon we share a daughter.

Craig has finally agreed to see me this afternoon, and although I am apprehensive, I am also relieved – this is a man I don't want to see fade from my life.

Oh, how I miss Emily even more at times like this! I know her advice may have been somewhat misconstrued ... but I know she would have made me laugh, and her heart would have been present in her words.

Perhaps she will come to me some day ... I wait eagerly.

Millie xo

Her eyes lingered over the flower-filled vase in the corner of the room. The shimmer of the paint she had used to colour the vase gleamed blue-green under the fluorescent lights above, and the flowers stood fresh and pink, their joyful presence ineffective at deflecting the heaviness that hovered over her heart.

A feeling of failure drifted through Bella's consciousness and settled in her stomach with an agonising twist. She recalled the day her angel had come through the veil to intensify the healing rays she had charged into the vase for her mother. And yet, here she lay in a bed of stiff white sheets in a hospital for the terminally ill. Her eyes skirted the floor. She gave an audible sigh and tried to gulp back the tears that sprang behind her eyes as she remembered the angel's words about freewill, *"Her health depends upon the consciousness she has of it, and the will she is free to manipulate."* – she didn't understand why her mother would want to leave her here alone.

There was no other family that she knew. Her parents had never spoken of other family members. When she had grown older and ventured to ask about relatives, her parents told her they had all passed. It made sense to her when she considered her parents' ages. They were much older than any of her friends' folks.

'You are our miracle child, Bella,' her mother would often chime.

Her father would chuckle from behind the paper that seemed almost permanently in front of his face. 'A gift from the angels to the world,' he would declare.

'Hmmm … never mind the world, Bella. You are a gift to us,' her mother remarked with a tender smile.

Her father lowered the newspaper to throw her a quick wink. 'This one will save the world. She's like Wonder Woman; our own little Wonder-Bella!' he beamed.

Bella almost lost the cereal in her mouth as she broke out into a fit of giggles. 'Wonder-Bella? Sounds silly, daddy,' she laughed.

'Yeah, Wonder-Bella. What's so silly about that? I think it has a nice ring to it.' Henry smiled at his young daughter.

After that conversation, Wonder-Bella had become the pet name her father favoured to call her, and she had quietly loved it.

Bella's thoughts were interrupted when Rose stirred. She reached out and clasped a hand over her mother's, squeezing gently with a smile as Rose's eyelids fluttered open to rest on her.

'Shouldn't you be at work young lady?' Rose croaked. Her thinning brows crossed momentarily before softening again.

Bella smiled. *Still as feisty as ever!* she marvelled. 'Mum, I'm going in a little later. I wanted to stop by and see you first,' she said.

Rose winced as she attempted to squeeze Bella's hand. 'You were here last night, Bella. You mustn't miss out on your shifts ... your work will help to keep you busy. Better than sticking around this old joint,' she mumbled.

'How are you feeling?' Bella leaned closer and kissed her mother on the forehead.

Rose eyed Bella thoughtfully. Her eyes narrowed when they settled on the dark circles that traced under her daughter's eyes. 'Better than you by the look of it.

Bella please, you need to look after yourself. Are you eating okay?'

Bella shook her head slowly. A look of bafflement plagued her face. 'Don't worry about me, mum. I'm a big girl.'

She avoided her mother's penetrating glare as Rose scrutinised her.

'Bella, I'll always worry about you,' Rose said quietly. She reached a bent finger under Bella's and lifted her daughter's face to her. Her chafed lips broke into a pliable smile, yet her eyes fused with concern as they searched Bella's features.

'I know you are finding this hard, Bella, but you are stronger than you realise.' She gave a rueful cackle. 'You are Wonder-Bella, remember?'

Bella's eyes brimmed with the salt of the tears she had fought hard to contain. Her smile was meagre as she succumbed to the inevitable flood that would smear her face.

'You are my miracle baby – our gift from the angels. When I leave this old and tired body, it doesn't mean I will leave you, do you hear me? I will never leave you alone, I promise,' Rose uttered.

Her voice broke with the last of her words and she beckoned her daughter closer. Bella fell into her arms like she had a thousand times before. Her body shook against the slender curve of her mother's shoulder and trembled within the frail grasp of her weak arms as she sobbed harder than she had allowed herself since this illness had crept into their lives like a relentless vile stench.

Rose clung to her daughter with all her strength, rocking her gently and hushing her tenderly until her rattling body stopped shuddering and her cries grew silent.

Bella pulled away reluctantly. 'I'm sorry, mum.' Her head hung with the shame that fluttered through her body.

Rose smiled and wiped at Bella's tear-stained face with her crooked hands. 'It's okay, Bella. Now, why don't you go off to work; I have a full day planned ahead of me here,' she said with a playful wink. 'I think that male nurse, Jeffery, has a little crush on me,' she laughed.

Bella laughed softly. 'Okay, mum. I'll be back tonight. Would you like me to bring you anything?'

Rose nodded wearily. 'Yes, dear. Please bring me my good letter-writing set; you know the one with the gold edging and the butterfly background? I have a letter to write.'

Bella gathered herself up, her legs unsteady. She cast a surprised look at her mother. *Who would she be writing to?*

'Sure. Who are you going to write to?' she asked.

'Oh, I think I have to break the news gently to this nurse ... I am a married woman, you know,' Rose remarked as haughtily as she could.

Bella rolled her eyes and tusked. 'Okay, well I'll bring you your writing set. I love you,' she murmured, leaning to kiss her on the cheek.

'I love you too,' Rose smiled.

Bella turned and walked towards the door, pausing when her mother called out to her again. Her voice was so soft that Bella was uncertain if she had called out to her at all or whether she had been hearing things. She frowned.

'Remember when that lovely real estate man gave you that card, dear?' Rose said.

Bella nodded.

'Now is the time to make the call,' she murmured with a knowing smile. She fluttered the tips of her fingers in a wave. 'Bye dear.'

Bella drove from the hospital with an air of relief flooding through her. She shivered. It was cold out, yet she knew her shudders did not stem from the wintery chill. Willing the car heater to kick in and produce the warmth she longed for, she mentally shed the suffocating feeling the hospital evoked in her. At every turn she could feel death creeping in around her, and despite the growing speed of the car, she could not shake its unwavering claim on her mother.

'Noooo!' she screeched out loud to the gushing wind of the air vents.

A flat palm smashed against the steering wheel in an outburst of frustrated helplessness as she cursed death and its unavoidable obliteration. She drove on. She drove past the aquatic centre where she was to begin her shift. She drove with the warming air of the heated vents blowing over her yet doing nothing to ease the paralysing churn that knotted her stomach. She drove without a destination in mind, yet with every corner she took it seemed as if a part of her she was not privy to, knew her objective.

When the car finally came to a halt, she absently gazed through the windows at the grey day. Her eyes narrowed as she became aware of her whereabouts and recognised the bay; she was in Rockton, a town on the other side of Sydney. A town she did not know well. The ridge of her nose screwed up with the crease of her frown. *What am I doing here?* She had astounded herself. Pulling the black woollen scarf tighter around her neck, she opened the car door and braved the thick fog that shrouded the bay's edge like an entwining misted rope.

Bella drew in a quick breath of cold air that felt like a gentle lick of needles as it filled her lungs. She tugged at the scarf, bringing the warm fabric over her lips to soften her next breath and began to walk towards the old wooden wharf that stretched out over ashen choppy waters.

She stopped when she reached the wharf's end to lean against the rickety wooden railings. The fog curled around her and clung heavily over the relentless lapping of the water as it rocked against the thick wooden pillars that held up the wharf. She peered down and studied the green slimy moss that covered the submerged section of the pillars. She watched a small crab clambering over the crustaceans and barnacles that traced the pillar's surface as it made a desperate attempt to escape the rising tide.

She ventured down a row of slippery stairs that led into the bay and reached out for the crab. 'Come here crab,' she whispered.

The tiny crab crawled onto the sanctuary of her fingers. She watched the crab taking little tedious steps over her hand. She was mesmerised at its miniature shell and its bitsy legs, forgetting that she stood precariously on slimy moss-laden stairs. She wished with all her heart she could join the crab in its uncomplicated world of existence.

'I'd be careful down there if I were you. The tide is rising fast and those stairs are as slippery as hell.'

A woman's voice broke through her reverie. Bella turned with a jolt, causing the little crab to fly off her hand. She looked up with a frown and spotted the fiery dark stare of a mature woman staring down at her

disapprovingly.

Bella forced a smile. 'Uh, thanks,' she called, waving her hand briefly.

Her eyes fell back to the stairs, scouring for the whereabouts of the crab.

'I think it went that way,' the woman's voice boomed down towards her.

Bella's glance found the brightly cloaked woman pointing disjointedly somewhere beside her. She nodded towards the woman, hoping by the time she made her way back up the stairs that she would be gone. She searched once more, unsure why this little crab was suddenly so important to her; she just knew that it was.

A moment later she spotted her miniature friend safe and sound and crawling its way to the dry haven of a crevice between the wharf and the pillar. Relief flooded through her and a meek smile crept over her lips. *Death won't claim you today, little one.*

She turned on her heel to make her way back up to the wharf, pivoting just a little too fast as she did so and losing her footing on the slimy stairs. Hands flew about wildly as she grasped at the rusted metal poles that passed for handrails. She managed to take firm hold just in time and steadied herself while cursing under her breath.

'Oh my goodness! Would you please come up here now – you almost gave me a heart attack!' The woman bellowed down at her.

Bella looked up to her as she began the incline, holding the rail tightly. The woman stood bright as a beacon in an aqua coloured trench coat that cinched smugly at her waist with a hot pink sash. She wore a matching pink beanie that revealed wisps of red hair poking out from beneath it.

Bella smiled as she neared her. 'Almost gave myself a heart attack too,' she remarked.

The woman's eyes softened for a moment before the frown returned. 'What were you thinking going down there in such precarious conditions, sweetness? Those stairs aren't safe even on a fine day,' she said. The throaty husk of her voice pitched a little as pink gloved hands waved through the air to emphasise her point.

Bella could see the woman had been genuinely concerned for her safety, and a rush of guilt surged through her.

She shrugged. 'I don't know. I'm sorry if I upset you,' she said solemnly.

The woman's frown relaxed. 'Holly,' she said.

Bella's face lightened. 'Annabella. Please to meet you, Holly.'

They exchanged a grin.

'So, what were *you* thinking coming out here on a day such as this?' Bella asked curiously.

Holly leaned against the railing and stared out

towards the stretch of water. Her eyes glazed for a moment. 'Most people tend to avoid the bay in weather like this,' she said wistfully. A deep chuckle vibrated through her throat. 'I discover the bay's secrets in all types of weather.'

Bella followed her gaze. She could barely make out the heads that sanctioned the large bay in the distance through the fog. She took a gulp-full of breeze through her mouth. The air drifted and circulated through her lungs with the thick taste of salt lacing her tongue. She closed her eyes and smiled. For one sweet instant she pretended she was a crab. All tension and stress fell away and she allowed herself to just be in the moment. She became aware of the cool dense fog against her cheeks, and savoured the salty scent of the bay as it curled through her flaring nostrils.

'You see. You have discovered it too,' Holly said softly.

Bella opened her eyes and looked at Holly. A slow nod communicated her agreement. 'Thank you,' she said.

Holly grinned. A mischievous expression struck her pencilled brows. 'I have hot chocolate and cookies nearby. Come Annabella, I think that's enough secrets for one day.'

She hooped an arm through Bella's and directed her back towards the beach.

'You can call me Bella,' Bella said as they strolled together.

Holly grunted. 'Annabella suits me just fine,' she grinned.

Holly chatted away as they walked through Rockton's main road, treating Bella to idle tales about the locals they passed along the way.

'Oh, don't look now but here comes Mr Anderson,' Holly hushed discreetly. 'He is the father of one of my dearest friends. His story is quite interesting to say the least.'

Bella watched the tall man as he approached them. His shoulders were scrunched as he huddled against the chill, and his hands were hidden deep within his pockets. When he lifted his eyes, they found her instantly, as if drawn to her like a magnet.

Bella's gasp was swift when her eyes met his and she was surprised at the sudden lug of air trapped within her as she unwillingly held onto it.

'Good afternoon, Mr Anderson,' Holly said as they passed.

Glen dragged his eyes away from Bella reluctantly. 'Hello Holly. Enjoying the lovely weather?' he said.

He paused, gesturing towards the drizzling oyster-coloured sky with a half laugh. He looked back to

Bella with an odd expression crossing his face.

'Funny. I thought I knew every face in Rockton,' he said. Curiosity afflicted his voice as he tilted his large spiky head towards her.

Bella smiled uncertainly. 'Perhaps you thought wrong,' she said flippantly.

Her gaze fell to the pavement. *Damn I need some chocolate!* she thought as her stomach knotted and she silently cursed her response.

A wide grin appeared over Glen's features. 'Perhaps I did,' he chuckled. 'You seem so familiar though,' he added almost to himself.

Holly introduced them briefly then graciously ushered Bella down the road, muttering excuses about hot chocolate and escaping the cold.

Bella glanced at Holly. She screwed up her nose in puzzlement as she contemplated her reaction to the man who had briefly passed them by.

'So, what's the interesting story?' she ventured.

Holly grunted and her faced darkened. 'A story best not told, Annabella,' she said.

Bella noted the ominous tone in her voice, before peeping over her shoulder to catch a glimpse of Glen before he merged behind a group of people.

'Oh look, here we are!' Holly chimed.

Feeling somewhat confused and disoriented, Bella turned to face a heavy glass door that bore the inscription, "Holly's Art Studio". She stiffened and her mind began to whirl as her eyes tracked the lettering several times over. She looked at Holly who was watching her with amusement.

She blinked a few times. 'You're Holly?'

The woman grinned. 'That's what I told ya,' she chuckled. 'Come on, sweetness,' she said, pushing against the door and tugging at Bella's arm.

A warm rush of air drifted over Bella's face as she entered the gallery. She paused and her eyes widened with excitement. A demure scent of burning vanilla candles invaded her sinuses and her eyes rested on an elegant display of sculptures. Drawing nearer, she marvelled at the contrasting parade of graceful designs and rustic edges. There were fine bowls designed from coloured glass, wood carvings, bronzed figures and ceramic treasures; each piece appeared to command its own space, and each provoked an intimate exchange of emotion from her.

She lifted her eyes and smiled as she scanned the canvases and the sheer weave of fabric overhead that twinkled with little lights. She sighed audibly as she soaked in the elegance of the gallery. *I'm in heaven!*

'Annabella,' Holly's voice interrupted her reverie like an axe splitting through a log.

She was back to earth like a shot. For the first time since she entered the gallery, she noticed there were others in the large room. A young woman was perched behind a slim counter; she held a pen in one hand and was watching Bella curiously. Beside her a little girl appeared absorbed as she doodled intently upon the pages of a scrapbook.

Holly bustled towards her. She had removed her bright coat and Bella smiled when she saw Holly's attire beneath was just as vivid.

She caught Bella's hand and tugged. 'Come Annabella, meet Amelia and Arella,' she chirped.

Bella allowed herself to be drawn closer to the counter. She noticed the woman's face light up.

'Hello Annabella,' Millie greeted with a finger wave. She turned and gave the girl beside her a gentle nudge. 'Arella, this is Annabella.'

Arella dragged her eyes from the paper. She frowned briefly as she looked at Millie, who gestured towards Bella. When she turned to Bella, aquamarine eyes ignited beneath thick lashes and her little face broke into a wide grin. Bella caught her smile and returned it with infectious enthusiasm. She grinned at Millie and stared transfixed. For an instant she became aware of what felt like a sudden charge of electricity pumping through her, and the surface of her skin broke out in goosebumps.

'Hi Bella. Do you like to draw and paint like my mummy?' Arella quipped, breaking through her hypnotic trance.

Bella lugged her gaze from Millie's.

Arella drew a deep breath and spoke again before waiting for an answer. 'I like to draw and I love to paint and some day I'm going to be a famous artist like my mummy. Do you know my mummy is going to be in an important art magazine next month? They came here and they spoke to her and they took photos of her and her paintings. Her paintings are so special, she can even paint the Golden World – and she hasn't even been there. It's not ready yet but it will be soon! How great is that?' she gushed.

Bella laughed. A streak of delight drew across her face and for the first time in a long time, the heaviness in her heart elevated. 'That *is* great. I would love to see your mummy's paintings; would you show me?'

Arella jumped off the stool with a squeal of joy. Little legs skipped to Bella and clasped her hand. 'Oh yes, c'mon!' she giggled.

She hesitated as she glanced at Millie for acknowledgment.

'I have a quick meeting out back in the studio. Rella, I'll be back in ten minutes … be kind to Annabella's ears, okay,' she said, winking as she rose to her feet.

'Okay, mummy!' Arella piped, pulling on Bella's hand and leading her to the other side of the gallery where canvases adorned the walls and stood alone on the perch of cast iron easels.

Bella glanced back at Millie. 'Oh, call me Bella,' she called before laughing and allowing Arella to drag her away.

Chapter Seven

MILLIE GENTLY BLEW INTO THE MILKY LIQUID. She studied the small ripples that quaked over the hot surface as she continued to blow into her hot chocolate. The velvety liquid hastily became subject to her artist's mind, and images of billowing water curling over the tip of a glass flushed through her vividly. *Angels ...* she mused. *Oh, I could place a charming little cherub in a glass of cascading champagne!* The idea felt good to her.

A blank canvas on her easel beckoned. Her fingers itched for her paints and brushes. She was just about on her feet when a light tap at the door interrupted her intention. Craig's tall frame swallowed the crack in the doorway.

She brushed a long lock of dark hair behind her ear while allowing the tips of her fingers to linger within the wispy ends. 'It's good to see you,' she murmured.

Her fingers began to twirl.

A few long strides and he was near her. The scent

of his familiar cologne filled her senses, and for a moment all she wanted to do was fall into the security of his arms. Instead, her gaze fell and she began to purposefully focus on the dried-up splatters of paint that decorated the wooden floor. She could feel his eyes trail over her as if they caressed her skin with a dripping of honey.

'Millie,' he said.

She was surprised to hear no animosity clouding his voice. It was the raw emotion that drifted through his soft tone that tore her eyes from the floor.

He reached out and clasped her hands within his. 'I'm sorry for making you feel ashamed,' he said.

She shook her head. 'No Craig. I'm sorry. I shouldn't have let it get that far with Damon. Not before I squared things off with you … it just happened so fast, and …' she stammered.

Craig's chuckle stopped her short. 'You didn't do wrong by me. I've had a lot of time to think on this. On the contrary, you have always been upfront.' Shoulder-length curls draggled with the shake of his head over his black trench coat. 'It was me holding onto you – even though you were honest and broke off the engagement. I can't fault you, Millie. I did this to me,' he said pensively.

He squeezed her hands gently and when he smiled she recognised the melancholy in his eyes.

'I didn't want to let go of you,' he whispered. 'You

are like the spark in my soul.' He searched her eyes for resolution.

Without warning, Millie broke down into tears. 'Oh Craig!' she murmured between the sobs that caught in her throat.

She threw herself into his embrace while a flood of emotion overcame her. *I do love you! I do!* Her mind tangled with the words, yet she knew she couldn't say it out loud. It wouldn't be fair to him.

Craig stroked the back of her hair and held her close. She leaned against his chest and closed her eyes. The thump of his heart beat loudly in her ear with a consistent thud and as Millie focused her attention on the pulsation that resonated through her, she felt herself lull into a state of nostalgia. She wound her arms around him tighter and sighed. Letting him go was harder than she had anticipated, and part of her wasn't quite ready to loosen to thread between them. *But then again, part of me never will be ready to let him go.* How do you say goodbye to someone you still love?

She felt him stiffen under her embrace.

'Millie,' Craig mumbled.

He swept his lips over the top of her head and inhaled deeply before extracting himself from her arms. She caught the yearning in his eyes as she peered up to him. They stood transfixed in silence, neither of them eager to bring an end to their time together, yet there was an air of awkwardness that hung between them.

Craig spun on his feet and began to shuffle around the studio as if inspecting its contents for the first time. He cleared his throat. 'So, are you going to be with him now?' he said. He did not look at her.

Millie grabbed a fistful of hair. Her stomach churned with the answer she knew he didn't want to hear. When she didn't respond he paused his self-imposed tour and looked at her.

She nodded her head slightly. 'Yes,' she murmured.

He returned her nod thoughtfully. A shot of pain tore through his eyes and penetrated into her heart.

'Does he know about Arella?' he said.

She barely heard his murmured question over the plummeting of the rain that had begun to pelt against the windows and the tin roof of the studio. Her gut felt hollow and she turned away from him. More than anything she knew he was reluctant to dissolve from her daughter's life. More than anything she knew how much he had longed for Arella to be his own child.

'Not yet,' she confessed.

'You need to tell him, Millie,' he said.

His voice sliced through the guilt that smeared her thoughts.

She turned to meet his stare and offered him a timid smile. 'I know,' she said. Her expression creased with her frown. 'I know it will be hard for you ... I want you to know there will always be a place in Arella's life for you – if you'd like it, of course.'

'And yours? Will there be a place for me in your life?' he replied.

The intense longing in his stare was as transparent as a pane of glass.

Millie sighed. She became aware of why he lingered. She grinned as a flood of relief washed through her. 'Nobody could ever replace you,' she said.

She was as hesitant to see Craig disappear from her life just as he was reluctant to no longer play a part in hers. Perhaps she didn't need to say goodbye after all.

She grinned. 'Everything will be okay, promise.'

He approached and reached for her hands. His eyes appeared mellowed as they locked onto and searched hers. He gave her a gentle squeeze as they exchanged a thousand moments shared and treasured between them, and a golden thread of emotions elicited through their eyes in silence. The significance of their time together was branded on their hearts with a sacred mark.

A smile swept across his lips. 'I know, Millie-pie,' he murmured.

They dashed from the studio and through the back door

of the gallery as fast as they could, finding themselves drenched despite the short stint of rain that assaulted them.

'Craig!' Arella squealed.

Her little legs made rapid pace as she ran to him and flung herself into his waiting arms.

Millie watched them for a moment. A stab of nostalgia found her smiling when she noticed Craig's closed eyes against the unruly twist of Arella's dark hair.

Arella squirmed under his tight grasp. 'I missed you. Mummy said you've been very busy, but I don't like it when I can't see you,' she said.

Craig smiled. 'I'm sorry, Rella. I missed you too,' he replied, reaching into his coat pocket and pulling out a lollypop. 'Will this make it better?' he asked.

She began to sway in a half twist as she eyed the lolly pop. 'Hmm … maybe a little, thank you!' she said, accepting it.

She giggled. 'Come and meet my new friend, Bella. We're having hot chocolate and cookies!'

She flitted away from them, lollypop in mouth.

Millie and Craig walked to where Holly, Bella and Arella sat together by the shop front window. They had rearranged a few pieces of French provincial chairs to encircle a delicately crafted wooden coffee table laden with over-sized mugs of hot chocolate and fine boned china plates with cookies. The graceful sounds of Mozart drifted through the air in muted tones.

Millie grinned. 'Looks like we're having a mad tea party,' she joked.

When Bella glanced over her shoulder as they approached, Millie felt a jolt ripple through her body. She drew in a sharp breath and paused. Her brows furiously knitted together as she racked her brain in a muddle. *She's so familiar.*

Bella stood. She smiled at seeing Craig and walked towards them. 'Craig, hello,' she said.

Millie's frown deepened with the dredging blush that flushed over Bella's face. *She knows Craig?*

His face kindled as the two exchanged greetings and instantly fell into conversation. Millie left them to it and joined Holly and Arella at the tea party.

She gestured towards them. 'What's going on there?' she said to Holly.

Holly grinned mysteriously. 'The grand phenomena of synchronicity at its very best,' she rasped.

Millie scrutinised Craig and Bella before glancing back at Holly. 'How do you mean?' she said.

Holly clasped her long colourful beads and leaned in close. Her brown eyes twinkled. 'Don't you see what I see?' she whispered.

Millie took another look at them. She noted Craig's erect stance as he leaned in towards Bella and the animated glow in his warm eyes as he met her gaze. She noticed Bella grasping at her hair and gazing up at him coyly while they chatted about how she had come to be at the gallery. Each of them broke into laughter easily.

'She's an artist too, you know,' Holly said in a low voice in her ear. 'She crafts sculptures. Apparently, Craig had given her my card. She didn't call me though ... oh no, we met by chance down at the bay this morning, and ...'

Holly's murmurs fell muted in her ear as she continued to watch them. An awkwardness insinuated its way through her and she couldn't tear her eyes away from them. She was unaccustomed to the feelings that invaded her, and when she realised their origin was from a vivid spike of possessiveness, she felt bewildered.

She shook her head and turned away. 'We don't know this girl,' she said cynically.

It was Holly's turn to be astonished. 'Amelia! I am quite surprised. This is very unlike you indeed.'

Millie looked at her before lowering her head. 'I know. Give me a break. I guess I'm not used to this kind of thing,' she shrugged.

Holly chuckled. 'Everything will be okay, sweetness,' she said, gently patting her back.

Millie smiled to herself. *Hadn't I just said the same words to Craig?* she thought. She regarded her daughter who was immersed in her drawings on the floor near them. Paper, colouring books, scissors and markers were spread around her in an organised mess. Her dark hair fell to one side and swept over the floor with the small movements of her head.

Arella sensed her mother's eyes on her and turned briefly to look towards her. Her eyes sparkled with the dazzle of her smile before turning her attention back to her art. The gesture reminded Millie of her daughter's father.

She turned to Holly suddenly. 'Would you mind watching her for a couple of hours?' she said.

'Of course, sweetness. Where are you going?'

A wave of determination crossed her features. 'I have to go and tell Damon something I should have told him long ago.'

'Oh! Are you sure, dear?' she said.

She rose to her feet and leaned over to give Holly a light kiss. 'Yep, thanks Holly,' she said.

She had never been more certain of anything.

Millie took a deep breath before pressing the buzzer to Damon's front door. Since his return to Australia, she had not made the short distance to his apartment and knew he'd be surprised to see her.

She fidgeted about impatiently. Now that she'd

decided to tell him Arella was his daughter, every second seemed like an eternity.

'C'mon … c'mon,' she uttered, jamming the buzzer again.

This time she heard the fall of footsteps as they approached the other side of the door. A slight jingle of the safety chain met her ears and seemed to be a prolonged action. She rolled her eyes. She was ready to open her mouth and express her growing impatience with the opening of the door when she caught sight of an unexpected view.

She gasped. Words failed her.

The woman standing before her wore a slightly amused expression. She was much taller than Millie, and despite the cold wet weather outside, her long legs were exhibited in a short miniskirt and stiletto heels. Turquoise eyes creased under a mountain of make-up; her smile was aloof.

'You must be Millie,' she purred.

Even her voice is smooth, Millie thought with distaste. She nodded.

Wine coloured lips widened. 'Thought as much. I've heard a lot about you,' she said.

She filled up the doorway with the length of her body and made no move to budge. The perfect arch of her brows raised, and her smile widened as she flicked back her long mane of blonde hair and leaned on the door frame.

'You've just missed him,' she said coolly. 'He had an urgent meeting with another client.'

Millie's expression dropped. 'Oh,' she stammered.

The woman nodded and inspected her long, varnished nails. 'Hmm ... I know it may come as a shock, but he does have other clients that are just as important as you,' she said.

Millie's brows raised. 'I'm sorry, who are you?' she said finally.

'I'm Selina,' she said with a short smile.

The expression of puzzlement on Millie's face was obvious.

Selina made an audible "tsk" sound while her lavishly thick lashes squinted together. 'Selina. I'm Damon's assistant,' she said, emphasising her statement with an irritable shake of her head.

Millie's gave a look of mock surprise. 'Oh, Selina ...'

Selina gave a curt nod.

'Yeah ... that's right,' Millie threw her hands in the air. 'I did not even know you existed until now!'

Selina took a sharp breath. Her eyes narrowed.

She recovered quickly and smirked. 'Well, Damon isn't the type to kiss and tell. I like that about him,' she said.

Millie eyed her while she attempted to mask the heart that sank within her.

A hand grasped and tangled in a fistful of hair. 'I guess it's a trait that serves him well,' she mumbled.

She glinted with triumph. 'Can I give him a message for you?'

She straightened her amazon-like body and smoothed down imaginary creases in her pencil skirt. With an exaggerated flick of her long hair, she evened her head and directed her gaze at Millie expectantly.

Millie shook her head slowly. 'No. I'll catch him another time,' she said, turning to leave.

'Millie,' Selina called back.

She paused at the top of the staircase and reluctantly turned to look.

A broad grin appeared on Selina's face. 'The past has served its purpose and it's where it belongs,' she said.

'Oh, you've got that right,' she murmured. She turned again, and this time she wasn't stopping.

She couldn't get down the three flights of stairs fast enough. She burst through the big lobby doors with a wail caught in her throat and her heart seizing painfully. She bolted through the rain till she reached the sanctuary of her car, her rain soaked face merging with the salty tears that fell freely.

What was I thinking? How could I get this wrong ... again! Her thoughts were in chaos. She slumped back in her seat and closed her eyes. *I thought he wanted this? Had I misread him?* She wiped at her face with the backs of her balled-up hands and gazed up towards Damon's apartment through the constant stream of rain.

Damon had moved back into his parents' old apartment when he had returned to town the year before. It was the same apartment he had spent many years making memories as a growing child. He had mentioned his awkwardness being back in that apartment. He had told Millie that even though he was now there alone, he could still feel his mother's stifling intentions among the walls. Millie had nodded in understanding. It had always been a smothering space, especially to her. Recollections of his mother's hostile behaviour towards her had flooded her mind.

Her eyes settled on the balcony he had waved and hooted down to her a hundred times when they had been kids. It looked different now. She remembered all the pot plants that used to litter the balcony, and how lush and vibrant it was. She had always enjoyed searching for signs of Damon from the street among the bright green canopy of his balcony, especially in the late summer afternoons when the falling rays of the sun would bounce golden hues against the ample sea of jade, giving the greenery a lustrous glow.

The balcony, which stretched across the third floor, was now barren of life and appeared bleak, more so through the grey sheet of the rain that soaked it. Even still, when Millie looked up towards it, she saw the

affection in his eyes as if it were only yesterday he had stood there smiling down at her.

She closed her eyes again and steadied her heart. She couldn't really blame him; after all it had been her pushing him away since his return into her life. *What did you expect?* She scolded herself. *That he would wait around forever?* She frowned as she attempted to make sense of her relationship with Damon.

It was he who had waltzed back into her life without warning the year before and rattled her soul with the relentless noise of his presence. It was he who had captured more than just her heart before being whisked from her life when she had been pregnant with their daughter. It was he who despite the long hours she had spent finding a place to lock his memory away, still loved him with all the depth of her heart.

She shook her head and her eyes flew open. 'Yes! I did expect him to wait, damn it!' she cursed under her breath.

A loud boom against the car window startled her. She nearly jumped out of her skin, and when she turned towards the culprit that almost scared her to death, her face softened when she saw him standing next to her car. Damon smiled down at her. He was wearing no coat and he held no umbrella, yet he stood on the sodden road casually under an unbroken fall of rain as if the sun breezed gently over him.

Millie gave him a half smile before her eyes grew serious and fixed on his as a thousand words silently exchanged between them as they watched each other through the scattered drops that clung to the fog of the window. When the vapour of her breath against the glass hazed him into obscurity, she wiped at the window and flashed him a smile through the hole she had uncovered through the white foggy veil.

He laughed and stepped closer to the car. He leaned forward and pressed his nose to the window while his eyes rolled heavenward in mockery and a frown appeared over his face. He looked back at her and motioned her to join him. 'It's a lovely day for a walk!' he shouted through the rain.

Millie laughed with a shake of her head. 'You're crazy!' she shouted back through the window.

His lips curved into a smile while his eyes seeped into hers. 'So, come be crazy with me,' he called.

A moment of contemplation and she wound her window down a few inches. 'Why don't you go ask Selina?' she blurted.

He cocked his head to one side as the rain plummeted over the creases of his face. His dark hair appeared blacker than ever and slicked flat to his cheekbones and forehead, the ends constantly dripping from saturation.

He gave a slight nod in understanding. 'I don't think Selina is as kooky as you,' he grinned.

Millie scowled. 'Oh, I'm kooky now? Is that why you're with her, because she's not kooky?' she huffed.

Damon's smile broadened. Without warning he reached for the handle and yanked the door open. He grasped her hand and pulled against her resistance until she was out of the car and next to him in the rain.

She glared at him as best she could through the vigorous fall of water stinging her face. *Clearly, he thinks this is amusing,* she sulked.

Damon laughed.

Her glare deepened. 'I'm not a joke, Damon! Nor am I kooky!' she glowered, suddenly feeling like a child.

She turned from him to make a swift escape back to her car. He caught her arm and pulling her close, captured her in an embrace.

He met her glare. 'You are no joke, Millie-pie, but you are kooky,' he said.

Millie looked up at him through the fluttering squint of her water-logged eyes. Even in the exposure of the rain-storm, she recognised the tenderness in his gaze and her resolve weakened. In a frozen moment, she didn't feel the rain, and the swishing of passing cars fell unheard as she allowed her frustration to dissolve with the puddles at her feet.

She grinned up at him. 'Takes one to know one,' she murmured.

He nodded slightly as he lowered his lips to brush

over hers lightly. The tips of their noses nuzzled together and both shut their eyes to the outside world cascading around them.

For the first time since she had driven away blinded by tears six years ago to leave him on the sidewalk cradling an ache in his heart, they felt undivided. Days, months and years of silently yearning, desperate craving and learning to live without each other were bypassed in a matter of seconds and Millie could feel the wonderful thump of his heart rejoice with her own. And just as two diamond encrusted hearts came to meet again, so too did the beating of their hearts.

Chapter Eight

ACE GRUNTED IN FRUSTRATION. IF IT WASN'T enough that his body ached with tension from the long hours spent riding the east coast to Sydney, sleep also evaded him. Madison's incessant snoring wasn't helping either. He gave her a politely placed shove.

She made raspy sounds as she stirred in her sleep and promptly continued snoring.

'Madi!' Ace poked her arm.

Strands of wispy red hair flared with her breath as she stirred again. 'Hmmm ... what?' she murmured.

'Are you trying to cut down some trees or what?' he snapped.

'Huh?' she struggled to focus.

'You're snoring like a bloody trooper, woman. Turn over or something,' he grumbled.

Her eyes fluttered open. 'I'm not snoring ... my nose is just whistling,' she said.

Ace's eyes widened in the darkness. 'Seriously? Did

you seriously just say that?'

'Hmmm, what?'

Ace groaned loudly. 'Nose-whistling in your sleep is the same as snoring, sugar-puss,' he said.

She manoeuvred her body in an awkward roll-over and drifted back to sleep. A blissful silence filled the small hotel room, yet still he could not sleep. He threw the stiff blankets aside and went into the bathroom. Cockroaches scattered at the flicked of the light switch as he ambled up to the mirror. He examined two angry blotches fighting for a piece of his skin on the ridge of his nose. He cursed and screwed up his face as he studied the emerging pimples. If there was anything he couldn't tolerate, it was imperfection on his person. He stood back a little to gain a better view of his upper body. *Well, we're all in shape here*, he mused, admiring the taut pectorals. His gaze shifted back to his face, and as he studied the contours and edges of his features, it occurred to him just how much he resembled his father.

'Dad ... I wonder if I should visit you,' he said to the mirror.

He recalled the last time he had spoken to him only a few months before. He had cursed himself for days for making that call because he had again shown his father his weakness. Yet his father was the only person who could understand his struggles with the demon. A soft smile played on his lips as he remembered his father's

arms around him the night he had attacked his mother. He had felt safe and loved, and had his dad not shown up that night, he was unsure of what might have happened when Millie had arrived. Sometimes he cursed his father's presence that night, as it would have given him the opportunity to finish Millie off along with his mother. But other times he thought upon his presence fondly, because deep within him he knew he would not have hurt his sister that night. *Not that night.*

He remembered how he had rambled on the phone about the serpent slithering unseen among them before breaking into a gruelling howl. He recalled the concern and desperation in his father's voice.

'Well, we'll see, I guess … we'll see,' he said.

He left the bathroom with a sigh and climbed back into bed. He leaned over to kiss Madison's cheek; she smelled of sandalwood and musk. He drew a piece of her long hair under his nose. He liked her scent, and sometimes her smile almost made him feel happy too. But not as happy as Millie's smile used to make him feel when he was just a child.

Millie's hands fidgeted with her smile; her eyes darted away from him. She recognised the desire in his eyes, and it took all her strength to ignore the sweet tingling that settled over her nether regions each time she caught sight of his hunger.

Damon grinned over the candle lit table. 'Millie? Where are you?' he said.

More fidgeting. 'I'm here,' she smiled. 'The lobster was amazing.'

'You already said that; is everything okay?' he frowned. 'It's not Selina, is it? I swear, there is nothing between us, Millie. It was just a little fling, it meant nothing.'

Her brows heightened. 'You might want to let her in on that.'

She reached for the linen napkin on the table and began to fold it over and over until it was a chunky small triangle. They had been enjoying a quiet seafood dinner. Holly had taken Arella for the night. Millie hadn't told Damon about Arella that afternoon in the rain – somehow that piece of news wasn't a good fit with that drenched scene. Hence Holly had offered her this night of freedom. *Bless Holly*, she thought, and not for the first time; the woman was a gift and Millie appreciated her presence in her life. She motioned to a passing waiter for more wine. *Wine will help*, she thought to herself.

'She is well aware of where we stand,' Damon replied. He reached for her hand and lowered his tone. 'She knows I am in love with you.'

Yes, well; you may not be when I tell you about Arella. Millie smiled. 'Damon, I need to tell you something.' She drew a deep breath and looked around desperately for the waiter. *Where is that wine?*

Damon frowned. 'What is it, Millie? Don't tell me you don't feel the same?' he said with a tinge of alarm.

'No,' she said, shaking her head.

'No?' he sighed. He leaned back in his chair and studied her for a moment. 'No? You don't feel the same?'

She gave a half laugh. 'No … I mean yes, but before anything else there is something you need to know,' she said.

Damon leaned closer. 'I'm all ears,' he said.

'Ahh, the wine,' Millie smiled up at the waiter gratefully as her glass was refilled. She thanked him and took a hefty sip, prolonging the distraction.

It wasn't long enough though, and she debated whether she could string it out a little longer by taking another sip from her glass. Her thoughts were interrupted when Damon noisily cleared his throat.

'Millie?' he pressed.

She closed her eyes as she became aware of the quickening of her pulse. She took another breath and looked at him squarely. 'Arella is your daughter.' The words reluctantly spilled from her lips. *There I said it!*

She noticed the changes in his expression as the information seeped through him. He gaped at her as his face paled. Her heart thundered and she could barely breathe as she waited for him to say something.

Damon rubbed at his chin. 'The willow tree,' he said.

Millie nodded. 'The willow tree.'

'But that was so long ago and I left right away.' His face was a blend of emotions.

He picked up his glass and drained the wine before looking at her. 'Why didn't you tell me?'

'I did! Well, I thought I did,' she muttered, dropping her gaze.

His eyes glistened as the realisation dawned. 'The letter you gave your father to post,' he said.

She nodded. 'I thought you turned your back on us.' She felt tears flood into her eyes as past emotions rose to the surface.

'I would never do that!' he asserted.

Millie squared her chin as she looked up at him. 'Then what would you have done, Damon?'

'I would have come back!' he said.

Her eyes narrowed. 'Really?'

'Yes, really.'

Her eyes flashed with ire. 'Are you sure about that? Because from where I was standing, you never looked back,' she snapped.

Damon scowled. 'That's not fair. I tried getting in touch with you so many times; all I wanted to do was run back home and, so help me god, I would have been here in a flash if I thought you'd still have me!' He took her hands in his. 'Millie, I thought it was you that had turned your back on me.'

Her eyes misted over with tears. She remembered those days almost as if it were yesterday, and as her memory drifted to the uncertainty of that time, her chest seized with a terrible ache. *Why had my father interrupted our communication?* she thought for the thousandth time since she had discovered Damon's revelations. Her dark hair tumbled loosely around her face as she shook her head and sighed. After everything that had happened with her mother and Ace at the retreat, she had never found the time to bring it up with her father. In fact, the two had never discussed that night nor anything of significance since. Except occasionally about Ace. Their relationship, which was already fraying around the edges, had unravelled more since finding him and Ace at the retreat with her mother's lifeless body. *Perhaps it's time to have a long overdue talk with my father.*

Millie shuddered and pushed away the tide of discordant thoughts. *I should know better than to invite these feelings*, she scolded herself. She forced a smile. 'So, what now?' she said.

Damon grinned up at her. 'Now I get to know my daughter.'

Her expression softened. 'And she will finally get to know her father.'

He squeezed her hands gently. 'But tonight, we get to know each other again.'

Millie's heart did a flip as she noticed the excitement brewing in his eyes. She lowered her gaze and bit down on her bottom lip in an attempt to control the uptake of butterfly wings in her stomach. Suddenly, she felt like a teenager with a wild crush. How Damon still managed to evoke such feelings was beyond her, yet she enjoyed the buzz that trilled through her senses.

When he motioned a passing waiter for the bill, his voice became low and throaty, and he whisked her from the restaurant with an urgent intent. The cold night air hit them with a brittle blast, yet neither of them noticed the vapour of their breaths against the icy breeze, nor the escalating headiness of the wine. He clasped her hand firmly, leading her through the wet alleyway to the back lot where he had parked his car.

As they neared the car, Millie's breath hastened with every step. She was aware of his every move next to her, and her body responded like a ripened pear ready to be plucked and devoured. She could feel the swell of her nipples as they strained against her lacy bra with every heave of her chest; *And he's barely touched me yet!* she mused.

Her observations were hindered when he pushed her against the car. His hands lingered over her face as he leaned towards her, his parting lips finding her mouth with the release of a moan. His soft tongue was soft and hot as it probed around hers, and as his kiss deepened, it seemed to wrap around her own crucially. Millie felt his erection harden, even under the layers of clothing that were meant to keep them warm. She tried to move, to say something along the lines of going back to her apartment but she felt as if she were captive to an invisible thread. She snaked her hands under his shirt and found his smooth hot skin. She pressed her mouth on his while exploring the hard contours of his chest before slipping her hand down to firmly clasp his shaft. He groaned, then suddenly moved away, his breath almost whooshing as their eyes locked with only the scant glow of a lone street light to burnish their vision.

She met his gaze with the gold flickering hunger of her own. A small shriek of surprise rose from her throat as he lunged for her, and almost brutally turned her around. He pressed against her, meshing to her body while he shimmied the skirt of her dress and skimmed his hands roughly over her thighs. Moist lips left a trail of seductive promises on her neck, and when he bent her over the bonnet of the car, she thought she might explode from the excitement sweeping through her. She willingly succumbed to the delicious throes of lust as his fingers tangled in her hair and his erection burst between her parted legs. She moved her hips to draw him in and out with the urgent thrusts of his passion until her climax shattered and quaked through her body with his deep penetration.

Damon groaned and encircled his arms around her. He nuzzled her neck and nibbled on her earlobe. 'You still take my breath away, Amelia Anderson,' he murmured.

Millie leaned back into him and grinned while still panting from their lovemaking. 'And you just took mine,' she laughed.

It was then she became aware of the wintry air numbing her fingers and her damp clothes from the wet car. She shivered slightly. 'Let's go home.'

Millie stifled a yawn and smiled dreamily. It was way past her bedtime and sleep beckoned her, yet she was determined to stay awake just a little longer. They were snuggled in her bed sipping on hot tea and recouping from a night of intense lovemaking.

Damon groaned as he reached for an exposed nipple when she placed her mug on the bedside table. She brushed his hand away playfully. 'I think we're all caught up for one night, lover,' she giggled.

He grinned and eyed her over lazily. 'We'll never catch up; in fact I might have to quit my job and dedicate all my time to catching up with you – lover!' he winked.

'No hurry; we have the rest of our lives,' she said.

'That's right,' he said, pulling her in for a kiss.

She rested her head on his chest, revelling in the comfort of his arms around her. Oh, how she had missed him! She gave a contented sigh as her head rose and fell with the gentle heave of his breathing. The beat of his heart filled her awareness with the blissful euphoria in which she found herself captive. All was perfect in that moment; they were cocooned in her bed together with the beginnings of another rainfall smattering against the window, and she knew she had discovered a piece of bliss along her path.

Millie looked at him. 'I remember the way you made me feel when we were teenagers. It wasn't like this.' Her face grew contemplative. 'It's different now; we're different. Oh, I just realised, we're adults now!'

He smoothed her hair from her face. 'Some things have not changed,' he said.

'Like what?'

'Like the way your eyes flash with gold when you're angry or passionate, or the way you twirl your hair when you're unsettled … and mostly; the way you make me feel,' his eyes held hers. 'I remember you. I remember everything about you,' he whispered.

Millie nibbled on her bottom lip. Her eyes swam with the brim of emotions and she lost herself in the blue lagoon. 'I love you,' she said.

'I love you even more,' Damon murmured.

They spent the following hour discussing Arella. Damon wanted to know everything about his daughter; from the event of her birth through to the present day. Millie dug out all the photo albums and handcrafted school relics, and proudly presented as much of Arella as she could, careful to not leave out any important details.

'She's just like you; especially when she can't get what she wants – she has your droopy-eyed pout!' Millie laughed.

'Since when do I do a droopy-eyed pout?' he demanded.

She threw a pillow at him. 'Since as long as I've known you, mister.'

He caught the pillow with a pout limping his expression before they both fell into laughter.

'I can't wait to meet her tomorrow,' Damon said.

Her eyes glazed. 'I need to prepare her first; she has no idea … and she can be very sensitive. Tomorrow I will tell her, and Monday after school we will all have dinner together. How does that sound?' she said.

'You're right. I'm just eager to meet her – like yesterday! But I'll wait till Monday,' He planted a light kiss on the tip of her nose.

She smiled hesitantly. Now she just needed to work out how to break the news to her daughter.

Bella groaned as she hit the wet piece of clay with a balled fist. Her teeth clenched hard as she vented her resentment on the would-be sculpture. When she had given the clay a few good rounds, she fought to gain her breath as the tears rolled over her cheeks. She had arrived home from the hospital feeling the usual spike of grief wrenching through her gut, and although she was always careful not to allow her mother to see how hopeless the situation made her feel, even then she knew she had failed. Her mother was deteriorating before her eyes and she was powerless to do anything about it. Bella noticed the foul stench of sickness clinging to her mother more and more, and she knew it would grow until it claimed her completely.

She cradled her face in her hands and succumbed to the anguish she fought to contain. She wished for relief with all her heart. A slight shiver ran from her neck down her spine. She shook her head, ignoring the tingling sensation and her angelic visitor.

'Bella,' a soft voice called.

Bella shook her again. 'Go away!' she shrieked.

She felt the angel's presence linger for a moment before finally dissolving and leaving her alone again. She sighed. *Great, now I get to feel guilty over that too.* She knew her angel wanted to help her but she was so caught up in the despondency of recent events, she could not accept her angel's aid.

She ambled back from her studio to the house just in time to hear the doorbell chime. She languidly made her way down the hall and opened the door to find Craig clutching grocery bags.

He grinned. 'Have you been fighting with your sculptures?'

'Huh?' she mumbled.

Craig chuckled. 'By the looks of it, I'd say the sculptures won.'

'Oh,' she gasped, realising how she must look after pummelling the clay and smudging it over her face when she cried.

She began wiping at her face with the backs of her hands, which only served to spread the brown clay further.

'You look like a little puppy dog,' he said.

'Thanks; what are you doing here anyway,' she huffed.

'Well, a little birdy told me that a little puppy dog might like some company and a home-cooked meal,' he said.

Her eyes narrowed.

'I make a great chicken and leek pie – Arella can verify that. Should we call her before you throw me

away?' he joked.

She gave a little laugh. 'Did my mother put you up to this?' she said.

Whiskey eyes settled on her. 'She may have, but I didn't need much of an excuse. I could really use some company tonight too,' he said.

She allowed a smile to break her despondency. 'I could too,' she conceded, stepping back to let him inside. 'You know where the kitchen lives. I'll just run upstairs for a quick shower.'

'Great! Be prepared for the most delicious pie to ever hit your dinner plate.'

'Can't wait!' She was already half way up the flight of stairs. She paused and gazed down at him. 'Oh Craig, thank you,' she added.

'My pleasure,' he said.

She climbed the rest of the stairs to her bedroom with a small smile lingering on her lips. A little flush of excitement involuntarily sprang and rushed through her; relief was already finding her.

Chapter Nine

August 17, 1998

Dear Journal,

Oh, how sweet life is when love comes to town!

Okay, so with all that I've experienced, I am completely aware that ultimately, love is found from within; but when love is all and God is love, isn't it natural that we reach out to give and receive love from one another?

Let me have this moment of rejoicing! Let me revel in the love from another — and not just any other; my deepest other.

I feel unity with all of life!

My body has come alive with the sweetest sensations, and I'm almost feeling like a teenage girl.

Yesterday, I sat with Arella and told her everything – well almost everything. She didn't need to know about the sexy car episode or what happened when we got back home, but I did tell her the story of Damon and me. For a 5-year-old, she took it pretty well. Considering the subject hadn't been discussed at length in the past. Her response? "I know mummy, and I've been waiting to meet him." A typical Arella response.

I love that girl so much.

So, today I have a cherub painting to tackle at the studio, and Bella is bringing in some of her sculptures – which I am looking forward to seeing.

After that, dinner with Arella and Damon. I think I will cook something special; lasagne and passionfruit tart.

It's going to be a wonderful day!

Millie xo

A loud knock at the door rattled Glen's senses. He groaned and pulled the pillow over his head. 'Go away,' he grumbled.

Another blast jolted the door and shattered the last of his slumber. He mumbled under his breath as he dragged his tired body from the bed and shuffled to the front door. *Didn't people know it was rude to knock on doors so early?* He had worked a double shift the night before, and wasn't accustomed to morning house callers.

He threw the door open and struggled to focus on the two women who had interrupted his sleep. 'Yeah,' he said, rubbing his eyes and yawning widely.

The women were miles apart in age, yet they appeared to be dressed in similar conservative attire. Each held a pamphlet in their hands.

The older woman smiled. 'I'm sorry for interrupting you, sir. We are from the United Church and calling for donations. Have *you* found God in your life?' she said while offering him a pamphlet.

Glen frowned and took the brochure. He studied it for a moment before looking back at them, noticing the shocked expression frozen over the younger woman's face. *She couldn't be more than eighteen*, he thought dismissively.

'Umm … look, I just woke up from a late shift. Let me get my wallet and then you'll let me get some sleep, yeah?'

The older lady noticed the smirk that had grown over the younger woman's face. She followed her gaze and gasped when her eyes settled on Glen's crotch.

A bony hand clasped at her chest while the other snatched the pamphlet from Glen's hand. 'That won't be necessary!' she snapped.

She grappled for the younger woman's arm and tugged her forcefully away as they made for the porch steps. 'You … you pervert!' she hissed, pointing a crooked finger at him.

The young woman turned and flashed him a wide grin before she was whisked away down the street with her companion ranting beside her.

Glen watched them for a perplexed moment. He knew he didn't look his best, but what could they expect when calling on people on the early hours of a Monday morning? He shook his head and closed the door. It was then he glanced down and saw his morning glory protruding like a gallant sword through the slip in his pyjama pants.

He rubbed a hand over his spiky hair with a half chuckle. 'Oh well, I guess that takes care of that,' he shrugged, then headed for the bathroom.

He had just finished splashing cold water over his face when he heard another knock on the door. He grabbed for the towel and buried his face against the stiff starchy fabric, *Argh! She's comes back for a second round;*

what is it with these church people? he grumbled silently as the second knock rattled louder through the hall.

'I'm coming, I'm coming,' he sang out, heading for the front door and taking a quick peek downward to be sure there would be no inordinate display this time.

However, when he opened the door for the second time, his jaw dropped and his eyes stretched. It wasn't the church women calling to hurl abuse at him but his son. A wary smile erupted on his face.

Ace grinned broadly. 'Hi dad!' he exclaimed with a sweeping movement of his arms. He chuckled. 'Bet you weren't expecting to see me this morning.'

Glen recovered quickly. 'Good to see you, Ace,' he said, then turned to eye the redhead next to him. 'And which lovely lady have you brought home to meet your old man?'

Ace encircled an arm around Madison's waist. 'Meet Madison; the apple of my eye,' he said.

She burst into laughter. 'Oh, you are so sweet my Ace of games,' she gushed with the flutter of long lashes.

Glen and Madison exchanged polite greetings before all three fell into an awkward silence. He watched her as she clasped onto his son's arm possessively and pressed her bosom against him. He tried to ignore the slight alarm that stirred in him; he never had a thing for redheads.

Ace extracted himself from Madison's hold and

leaned in to grasp Glen in a bear hug. 'It's good to see you, dad,' he mumbled in his ear.

Glen slapped Ace's back affectionately, and returned the hug. It was then he spotted the green stone that hung between Madison's plunging V-neck sweater. He shuddered and felt himself go rigid as Ace stood back and looked at him.

'Everything okay, pop?' Ace asked.

Glen nodded. 'Sure, come in,' he said. He forced a smile and glimpsed the grin that spread over Madison's face as they entered his house.

It was rare to feel uncomfortable around another person, yet as much as Glen tried to shake off the unsettling feeling that Madison evoked in him, he couldn't. He fiddled about in the kitchen making coffee and eggs while she and Ace canoodled. He stole a glance at them and frowned. She was tracing a finger over Ace's thigh while whispering something in his ear that provoked a sly grin over his son's face. *Trouble*, he thought, turning back to the eggs. He didn't know what she was up to yet, but even before he had spotted that green stone, he knew her intentions were not sincere.

She saddled up next to him. 'Hey Mr Anderson,

would you like some help?' she said sweetly.

A shot of pain sliced through his head and he looked at her coldly. 'I got it, thanks,' he mumbled.

She reached over him and picked up a hot mug of coffee, brushing her breasts against his arm as she did so. She paused and searched his eyes with her own. 'Are you sure?' she teased.

His eyes dropped to the cold green stone pressing on his arm, and it took all his strength to contain the impulse to push her away. *Preferably out the front door*. He stepped away. 'Positive,' he said.

She smiled and cocked her head to one side. 'You know him well, don't you?' she said.

Glen eyes hardened. 'Not anymore,' he said.

'Well, okay,' she chimed, and sashayed back to the table.

They ate breakfast while Ace spoke about the land he had been working up north.

'I have work lined up when I return to Queensland. They have offered a good wage and the farmer's wife can cook real well,' he said.

He looked at Glen thoughtfully as he munched the last of his toast. 'Plus, they're easy to work with up there; they're all a few cards short of a deck, if you know what I mean.'

Madison laughed and started to stroke his hair. 'They're not as clever as *my* Ace of games ... not once have I seen a worthy poker-face in that crowd!' she winked.

Ace grinned and pecked her nose with his lips.

Glen glanced away before his appetite was ruined.

Ace chuckled and gestured around the kitchen. 'Dad, when are you going to sell up and get yourself something better than this old dump?'

He noticed the garish expression over Glen's face and grew silent.

'Never. I won't leave them,' he grunted.

'Leave who?' Madison piped.

He gave her a condescending glance as he stuffed more eggs in his mouth. 'My mother and my first wife,' he said.

'Millie's mother?' she said.

Glen ignored her and looked at Ace. 'When are you going to patch things up with Millie?'

His eyes softened. 'Please dad, I need some time. I'm trying to do the right thing here … I'm working and getting myself together.' He gave Madison's hand a squeeze. 'And I have a good woman beside me now.'

Glen scowled. 'Ace, we need to talk privately,' he said.

Ace nodded. 'Okay, we can do that. Madi can go out for a walk around town for a while,' he said, turning to her. 'Would you mind? There is a great ice-cream shop by the bay. I know how you love ice-cream even when it's cold out,' he teased. 'Besides, maybe you can find us a suitable car to drive back in?'

Madison sighed. 'Sure. I'll have peek around town.' She grinned as she glanced at Glen. 'Ice-cream is always best eaten when it's cold out,' she said.

'I bet you couldn't melt ice-cream even on the hottest of days,' Glen mocked.

Bella's blonde locks swayed with the beat of the radio as she sang along with Lenny Kravitz. She was on her way to the gallery with a few carefully wrapped sculptures she had stowed in the back seat, and to her surprise she was feeling more upbeat than she had for a while. Her green eyes crinkled at the corners as a smile swept over her face. It hadn't gone unnoticed that her spirits seemed to lift whenever she saw Craig. A tingle of delight shimmied through her as her thoughts turned to Saturday night.

By the time she had showered and dressed, a delicious smell wafted through the townhouse and lured her to the kitchen. The combined odour of bacon, garlic and leeks tantalised her tastebuds as it sizzled in a pan on the stove. She noticed Craig about to add the chicken to the mixture, and rushed over to stop him.

'Wait!' she demanded, then reached in to pluck out

a few crispy pieces of bacon.

Craig watched her with amusement as she devoured the bacon and flashed him a grin. He went to add the chicken again, and this time she grabbed his arm.

'Wait! Just one more bit,' she said.

'Aww, c'mon!' he groaned, 'there will be none left for my pie.'

Bella shrugged as she stuffed more of the bacon mixture into her mouth. 'You still have the chicken,' she said. The last piece of bacon missed her mouth, and fell down her top.

Craig burst into laughter when her face screwed up as she looked down her blouse.

'Need some help?' he teased.

She fished out the piece of bacon. 'Nope, got it,' she grinned.

Craig turned to the chicken and continued cooking. 'Wait till you see what we have for dessert,' he said.

Bella's face lit up. 'Oh, chocolate?'

He nodded. 'Not just any old chocolate; triple chocolate layered mousse cake,' he said.

She groaned in delight and poured them each a glass of wine. 'Why are you so good to me?' she said playfully.

He left the pie mixture to simmer and edged near her. 'Because you remind me of colour, and I like you,' he said, reaching for the wine.

She gestured with a tilt of her glass. 'Well, here's to

liking colour and people,' she said. Her expression grew thoughtful. 'What colour do I remind you of?'

He gave her an enigmatic smile as he studied her. 'A lovely pink-rose colour,' he said.

'I always liked pink roses,' she said.

They spent the rest of the evening talking, eating and enjoying the wine. By the time she had eaten a hefty slice of the cake, she held her stomach and groaned. 'I feel like Buddha!' she jested.

Craig wiped a crumb of cake from the corner of her mouth. 'A pink-rose Buddha; now that's something to behold!' he chuckled. He searched her face. 'You are something to behold.'

Her eyes dropped and her fingers twisted in her shoulder-length hair as her heart skipped a beat. When she looked back up at him, her full stomach fluttered when she saw the desire his eyes revealed. *What is it with this guy?* she wondered. She had found him attractive the moment they had met, yet the way he made her feel was much more than attraction; *Something more along the lines of affection,* she pondered. That didn't make sense to her considering her life was a mess lately. Surely there was no room for new love. *Was there?*

She didn't have time to think more about this, because before she could utter a response, he leaned in and pressed his lips against hers. His lips felt warm and soft as they lingered on hers and the fragrance of his spicy cologne flooded her senses. Suddenly she felt light-headed as a mixture of excitement and fear spiralled through her mind. She wanted to pull away. *This is going too fast!* – Yet the fluttering in her heart seduced her along with the growing fire in his lips as she found herself responding in a way that surprised her. And the world fell away.

He caressed his thumbs against her cheeks and pulled away slightly, their foreheads touching as their breath still mingled.

'You even taste like pink roses,' he said.

Bella grinned. Her body was filled with the warmth of his kiss and each stroking movement of his thumbs on her cheeks sent fireworks exploding down her spine. 'You taste like honey,' she said breathlessly.

He closed the gap between them and when he kissed her again, his lips crushed hers with lust. His tongue entwined around hers. She felt as if she floated on air, and the mood was sprinkled with magic as they invaded each other intimately for the first time.

Bella's thoughts returned to the present as she pulled her car up in front of the gallery. Craig was a wonderful man, and a skilled kisser. He made her feel lighter; it was as if the burden of her worries suspended when she was with him. He saw life the easy way, and she loved that about him. She was curious that when the time finally came, what kind of lover he would make. She and Emma had discussed this observation at length over the phone the moment Craig had left that Saturday night.

'Hi Bella,' Millie called, opening the gallery door. She walked to the car. 'Let me help you with your sculptures. I can't wait to see them!'

'Hey Millie – thanks.' She handed Millie a sculpture as they unloaded the car, making several trips back and forth.

Once inside the gallery, Bella hesitantly unwrapped each sculpture. *Oh, I hope she likes them*, she fretted.

Millie's delighted cries as she spied each piece revealed her appreciation as she marvelled at the delicately crafted models. When Bella unwrapped the last sculpture, Millie gasped as she regarded it with mouth agape.

Bella frowned. 'What?' she asked. *Is there something wrong with this one?* she wondered. The cherry lips of a cherub smiled dreamily as the tiny angelic creature leaned against a froth of silvery bubbles that overflowed from a glass of champagne; it was her most recent piece and she was proud of this one.

Millie's eyes lit up as she grasped Bella's hand. 'Come with me!' she said.

She led her through the back door of the gallery, through the short narrow path of the back alley and into the studio, stopping only when they came to a canvas perched on a paint-splattered timber easel.

As Bella peered at the canvas, her hands flew up to her mouth. The painting was the exact replica of her newly moulded cherub sculpture; even down to the sleepy grin playing over the creature's lips and the shimmer of the bubbles that lapped over the long stem glass.

'Oh my god! How is this possible?' she said, turning to Millie.

Millie shrugged. 'I don't know.'

'But when did you paint this?' she said.

'I've been working on it for a few days ... you?' Millie asked.

'Same – it's kind of bizarre.'

They stared at each other with astonished expressions and Bella could feel the tiny spread of goose bumps as they fleshed across her skin. It was almost as if Millie's eyes reflected her own; they seemed to visualise the same way.

'Do you talk to angels, Bella?' Millie ventured.

'Yes,' Bella nodded.

'Me too,' Millie whispered.

Bella was completely floored. She had spoken to no-one about her angelic experiences, expecting people to think she was crazy. And now, this woman, who felt so familiar, had painted her exact sculpture and was talking about visiting angels! She trembled as an electrical current ignited and buzzed through her while she noticed the same seemed to be happening to Millie. A radiant light gracefully bounced over and between them, and Bella could barely believe her eyes. Millie appeared angelic as the light enfolded her in a gentle glow.

Millie smiled as she extended her hands towards her. Bella lifted her hands too and when their fingers touched, a sphere of white light intensified and blazed over their hands as if uniting them. A tingling sensation ran up Bella's fingers and trickled exquisitely through her body. She returned Millie's smile as she felt a calmness permeate her. She noticed an image of opaque coloured wings appear and extend from Millie's back. The wings were elegant and engulfed in a glimmering haze. It was the most beautiful vision she had ever seen. She gulped and blinked in disbelief, but she had no time to question what she saw as Millie's gesture summoned for her to look over her own shoulder. She twisted her head slowly, feeling as if she was captured in a wondrous dream that she didn't want to end. And when her eyes looked behind her, she gasped at the delicately placed wings that unfurled from her own back and hovered behind her.

Bella blinked hard. She swayed from side to side and twisted around to get a better view of her wings. They differed from Millie's in that they were a soft pink colour with the edges crusted silver. *They are magnificent*, she thought. Her mind slowed to a serene melody, and she was barely able to comprehend the phenomena taking place. She took a breath and closed her eyes as she felt all tension dissolve from her, leaving a pleasurable perception of peace in its wake.

'Wow!' she whispered.

'Wow!' Millie whispered back.

In moments the visionary wings softened with the dimming of the light until they both diffused altogether. Millie and Bella exchanged looks of awe, their eyes conveying a thousand words that neither of them could find on their lips, yet a profound awareness struck them and they both understood the gravity of what they had just shared.

Bella's light laugh broke through the silence. 'So, what was that?' she exclaimed.

Millie wandered to a stool and sat down. 'You must be a descendant of an angel, Bella,' she said.

Bella gaped with her mouth wide open. 'Say what?' she laughed. 'No … my parents are no angels! I mean, they are lovely but they don't have a set of wings that just randomly appear out of nowhere.'

Millie shrugged. 'You never know for sure.'

Bella's brows furrowed. 'I think I would know that! How do you know about this anyway? It's happened to you before?' she said.

Millie nodded. 'Once before. My birth mother is an ascended angel. She no longer exists on the physical plane, but she is teaching me to use these gifts.'

Bella watched Millie with interest, and waited for her to continue.

'Okay, so here is what I know – the Ascended

Angels are like God's guardians to the earth. Each breath of God that comes into physical form – humans – come to earth to experience through their senses. To sift through our desires and learn to think and act from our higher beings rather than from physicality. Ultimately, the path of freewill will eventually lead us back to God – to the light. The ascended path.'

'So, have you reached this stage? And why do we have wings?' Bella quizzed.

'I am still on the learning path. Sometimes I think I've got it sorted and other times, not so much,' she shrugged. 'The wings are your gift to the world. You'll learn how to use them with time,' she said.

Bella went silent and began to amble around the studio looking at Millie's paintings.

'There's something else, Bella,' Millie said.

Bella paused and turned to look at Millie.

Millie's expression became serious. 'The serpent god; Apepsis. He seeks to populate the earth with his will, and uses humans that are vulnerable to his advances by instilling his dark force within them. These people are dangerous. They kill without conscience and their mission is to wipe out the Ascended Angels; and those of us that are angel descendants – or have wings!' she winked.

Bella's jaw dropped and the lines above her nose etched deep. 'Are you serious? This sounds like ... like,'

she stammered.

'Like a fairytale,' Millie said.

'Yes!' Bella asserted. She pushed her hair from her face as she attempted to grasp Millie's words along with the mystical encounter they had experienced together. *Is this really happening?* she wondered. Her eyes settled on a canvas that portrayed golden-crusted pyramids, a shimmering blue lake and majestic unicorn gates. A vividly striking sunset cast heavenly hues over the canvas.

When she glanced back at Millie, she wore an expression of nostalgia. 'I've been to this place,' she said, gesturing to the painting.

The string of bells on the gallery door chimed loud, breaking through their discussion.

Millie rose to her feet. 'The Golden World,' she said, turning to head for the gallery.

Bella trailed her with an air of elation sweeping through her, yet her stomach flipped with uneasiness. It was then she knew there really was truth to Millie's words. It was then she somehow knew her life was about to be turned upside down.

Chapter Ten

WHEN THEY RE-ENTERED THE GALLERY, Millie caught sight of a woman lingering in the front corner among the French provincial pieces and the scented candles. She seemed particularly interested in a sculpture of a man and a woman leaning towards each other and joining at the lips. The carefully carved wooden couple was connected from the bottom down in a circular twist.

Millie approached behind the woman. 'The artist calls it "Eternal Unity". It symbolises fertility and relationship energy-balance and it's quite lovely,' she said.

The woman turned around. Her dark eyes flashed as she smiled. 'It really is something, pussy-cat,' she said.

The woman's voice was gravelly and rugged, and fell on Millie's ears with a shudder. Her pulse began to race on high alert. She eyed her cautiously as she noticed the cloud of dark haze drifting over the woman like a dreary shadow.

She cleared her throat. 'Can I help you with

something?' she said.

The woman tilted her head as if in deep thought. The red shock of her curly hair dangled and brushed against her black attire. 'Oh, that depends.' She lifted a silvery-ringed hand to clasp the pendant that hung from her neck and began to meander through the gallery.

Millie followed her discreetly as her stomach began to churn.

The woman paused in front of one of Millie's canvases. It was a bleeding oil colour of a willow tree. Its long leaved branches were captured in a gentle sway and white dandelion thistles littered the scene like a mantle of snow.

The woman swung around to face Millie. 'You're Amelia Anderson, right?'

'That's right,' she replied.

'Thought as much.' Her eyes explored Millie for a moment. 'Oh look, you have fluff!' She reached out to dust Millie's shoulder.

Millie shrank back as the woman roughly groped at her shoulder, capturing a few strands of hair as she did so. 'Ouch!' she snapped.

'Oh my god; I'm so sorry! I was just trying to get the fluff off your shoulder but you moved,' she smiled.

Millie drew her cardigan tighter around her. 'It's okay. Is there something in particular you are looking for?'

She clutched at the pendant again. 'Do you have any snake art? I just love snakes.'

Millie's eyes dropped to the woman's hand that twisted the green stone between pudgy fingers. Her mouth grew dry, and for a moment she dared not breathe. She glanced over at Bella who was busy setting up her sculptures on a display shelf and appeared oblivious to their interaction. When she turned back to the redhead, she was watching her with a smirk.

'I'm sorry, we don't have snake art. You might want to try the reptile store across the street; you'll find snakes enough there,' she said, trying to keep her voice from quivering.

'That's too bad pussy-cat,' she hissed, retreating towards the gallery entrance before pausing to watch Bella setting up. 'Because snakes are much better than angels, and so much more interesting.' She leered over her shoulder as she pushed open the door. 'Maybe one day you'll realise that.'

Millie watched as the woman strolled down the street until her eyes could no longer follow her. She noticed her pass the reptile store without going in, and head on towards the bay. Millie pulled her woollen cardigan together until it wrapped snugly around her. However, no matter how tightly she held the soft stitches, she could not stop the incessant shiver that crept through her body like a minor earthquake. *Who is she?*

Why did she call me pussy-cat? Her thoughts spiralled. There was only one person who had ever called her by that name; and she was gone. Bella saddled up beside her and placed a hand on her arm, splintering her troublesome thoughts.

'Are you okay? You are as pale as a ghost,' Bella said.

She nodded slowly. 'Did you see that woman?' she said.

'The frizzy redhead?'

'Yeah,' Millie turned to face Bella. 'Remember how I told you about Apepsis instilling his will in some people? Well, she is one of them.'

Bella gasped. 'But ... how do you know that? She seemed nice enough,' she stammered.

Millie's expression was grim and her green eyes flashed in a golden ark. 'She knows we are connected with the Ascended Angels. Bella, we have to be careful now; do you understand?'

Bella's eyes widened. 'Okay, but I'm sure she was just checking us out, right? Nothing serious.'

Millie grasped Bella's arms firmly. 'You can never underestimate a sleeping snake; they can see with their eyes closed. I know them only too well,' she said.

'How well?' Bella ventured.

She sighed as she dropped her arms. 'Very well. I even love two of them,' she murmured.

'Oh my!' Bella paused in thought. 'Okay, listen. Let's

not get too carried away with all this; I'm sure we won't see that woman again. Geez, we just had the most awesome experience out there! Let's focus on that instead.'

She grabbed Millie's hand and pulled her towards her sculptures. 'What do you think?'

Millie chuckled. 'They look beautiful. You're right, I'm probably over-reacting,' she said, giving Bella a light squeeze. Their eyes locked. 'Thanks Bella,' she said.

Bella wrapped an arm around Millie and rested her head on her shoulder as they both studied the display. 'Thanks Millie,' she whispered.

Millie snuggled her head against Bella's. She absently looked over the sculptures while taking a deliberate breath. Bella's presence gave her a sense of warmth and a peace she could not explain, yet as they stood together looking over the beauty of the sculptures, and breathing in the aroma of scented candles that wafted through the gallery, she was unable to shake the feeling of dread that quivered through her and settled in her gut like a tightly woven knot. *There is a snake in town, and she slivered way too close for my liking.*

Ace sat on the cobblestone steps and looked over the unruly yard. His blue eyes furrowed with the frown that etched over his face. He had hoped his father had maintained the garden as they had done so together during his time at home. The weeds were beginning their relentless tangle through the flower beds and even poked between the cracks in the steps. He reached down and began to pull at the unwanted plants as he heard the thud of the back screen door behind his father.

He glanced at his dad as he sat down next him. 'Remember the time when we spent all summer out here clearing out the weeds?' he said, throwing a handful of shrubs aside.

Glen nodded and chuckled. He gazed out to the yard and his eyes glazed over for a moment. 'That was a good summer,' he replied.

'Yeah, until Millie dug up that damned box,' Ace scowled. He could feel his father's eyes on him as he clutched more weeds and pulled hard. 'Everything changed after that.'

Glen's sigh was heavy, yet he said nothing as he continued to observe Ace.

Ace tossed the plants aside again. 'Something else happened that day. I remember how scared I felt clutching Benny-boy and covering my ears while you and Millie went to battle. But when it was all over, I wasn't scared anymore; I was angry,' he said.

Glen squeezed his eyes shut for a second, and when he opened them again, they were filled with unspent tears. 'I know. I'm sorry; I should have been there for you, and I should have helped you overcome the darkness ...' His voice trailed and he brushed his eyes with the backs of his balled fists. 'Only, I didn't really know back then how to overcome him. I tried, yet I failed so many times. I can help you now though; I'm here now.' He awkwardly put an arm around his son.

'What if I don't want your help, pa?' Ace said.

Glen's eyes narrowed.

Ace gave a half laugh. 'I mean, I'm going well now. I'm better and I have kicked the dark force in the butt!' he joked.

Glen searched his son's face with deep furrows showing on his forehead. Ace noticed how worried he looked, and for the first time that day, realised how much his father had aged since the few months he had seen him.

'He's not so easy to shake, Ace,' Glen said gravely. 'I've known him only too well. My success in banishing him came from your sister's grace. She can help you too.'

Ace shrugged with a laugh. 'You don't need to worry. I've got this,' he said. He gestured to the yard and a lopsided grin emerged on his lips. 'A weed is a plant that has mastered the skill of survival; and I have too.'

His father stared into him and it took all his strength not to squirm under his penetrating gaze. *Geez, I wish he'd let up*, he thought. He concealed his annoyance while he pried himself from his father's arm and ventured down the stairs and began yanking out as many weeds as he could. 'Damn weeds,' he muttered.

'Ace!' Glen boomed.

Ace paused and squinted back at his father.

Glen rose and looked down at him. 'My father was not the kind of man I could ever turn to …' his voice trailed and he shook his head. He glanced up at the yard, his jaw squared. 'Watch yourself with the redhead,' he warned, then turned and disappeared through the back door.

Ace sighed with relief. He could barely endure the burden that entangled his father, and he was glad the scene was over. He turned his attention back to the weeds. Seldom had he heard his father speak of his own parents; the only thing he had ever really known about them was that they had lived in this house. *This damned house!* He brooded inwardly as his hands fought against the dense undergrowth with growing speed. Sharp branches and thorns scraped his knuckles and dug through his flesh, yet he was oblivious to the pain as his blood dripped and mixed with the earth. His chest tightened and his breath came fast as he fell to his knees panting. He clutched fistfuls of earth between his fingers while he attempted to tame the painful twist as it seeped into his awareness. His gaze turned slowly towards the giant avocado tree that stood fearless and noble at the side of the yard just as it always had. He was sure it was taunting him with its thick spidery branches and flourishing trunk. This tree held family secrets and had kept them safe for the longest time. He sneered at it. *Damned tree.* He rose to his feet and growled under his breath as he charged at the tree, swinging his arms through the air and repeatedly smashing balled fists into the solid trunk.

He paused and gazed up at the centre of the tree. Glittering streaks of winter sunlight bounced and frolicked over the lush leaves, giving the tree an animated sense of character. He was certain the tree was mocking him now. He grunted and whacked his shin against the trunk, slogging into it with his leg. Pieces of bark flaked off the tree, exposing sections of the sturdy fresh layer beneath it. Ace began to claw at the outer casing, frantically peeling and pulling the woody folds off the trunk. Splintery brown fragments jammed under his short nails as he grappled, yet he continued his mission to beat up the family-destroying tree until finally he saw the sap of the tree ooze and bleed in a thick brown trickle.

He collapsed to the ground and leaned towards the tree. Ignoring the throb of his bleeding limbs, he wrapped his arms around the bottom of the trunk and rested his face against the bumpy hard surface. There was a time he had loved this tree. He closed his eyes and thick tears rolled over his cheeks while visions of climbing the branches and picking its offerings filled his mind

with fleeting joy. There was a time when this tree had loved him, he was sure.

'Ace?' Glen called.

His father's voice cut through his reverie with a bittersweet sliver. He fluttered his eyes to focus on his dad who was looking down at him with puzzlement.

'It's okay, dad. I'm okay,' he replied, hauling himself to his feet. 'Just a bit of tree-loving, that's all,' he said, forcing a smile as he rose and walked past him.

'I'm going for a shower.' He called back before disappearing inside.

By time he had showered and dressed, Ace was relieved to see Madison had returned from her walk. He rushed to his old bedroom and threw a few of his belongings into a bag, then scampered to the kitchen to usher themselves out of the house and away from his father. Too many memories lived here, and stirred through him like a suffocating web. Besides, although he had welcomed the sight of his father, he was eager to put some distance between them. He wasn't ready for the truth his father had tried to reason from him, and he had discovered his father's presence had only served to evoke a conflicting struggle within him. He had come back to Rockton with a plan. He squared his jaw with conviction. *And I will follow through with the plan*, he resolved, pushing away the lingering perplexity.

'Okay dad, we're off. Gotta get on the road and pick up these supplies for old Glassop!' he announced while grabbing Madison's arm and steering her towards the hall. 'Did you find a van?' he murmured in her ear.

She nodded. 'I did real well,' she whispered.

He reached out to grope a breast as they ambled down the hall. 'Good girl.' He gave her a squeeze. 'I'll show you how good you are later,' he winked.

Glen followed them. 'When will you be back in town?' he asked.

'Dunno,' Ace replied.

Glen made grumbling noises behind him.

Ace smiled and paused at the front door. 'I'll try and be back soon; love you,' he muttered.

He leaned in to give him a swift hug. His father enveloped him in his arms and pulled him close. 'I love you too. Don't forget what I said,' he said gruffly, giving him a pat on the back.

'So long, Mr Anderson,' Madison chimed with a grin as she paraded to a big white van.

Glen grunted his farewell to her and looked back at Ace. 'I know it's hard fighting the demon inside, but you need to keep fighting it. There are people here that love you,' he said.

Ace chuckled. 'I told you, I'm good. Trust me,' he winked, and headed to the car.

He loaded his bike in the back of the van as carefully and as fast as he could. Once behind the wheel, Ace began to feel his breathing ease as his chest relaxed. The engine roared to life. 'Not bad; where did you get it?' he asked.

Madison laughed. 'Oh, I have my magic remember? Let's get out of this place!'

'Let's do that, witch,' he winked.

When he gunned down the street, he took a deep breath and smiled as he spied his father's figure shrinking in the rear-view mirror. He caught a glimpse of his eyes in the reflection as he turned the corner and levelled out in the next street. '*Turn from evil and do good, I beg you.*' Sheila's words popped up out of nowhere and bubbled through his thoughts. *No!* He shook his head, pushing the thought from his mind. '*There are people here that love you … Keep fighting him, Ace*'. His father's voice echoed in his head. *No!* He shook his head harder and turned up the radio. '*Keep focused, Ace. Power and riches await you.*' The forceful voice of Apepsis immersed itself in his mind and rooted into his consciousness. *Yes!*

Ace glanced back to the small mirror. He remembered when his eyes were coloured like the sky and saw enchantment in every corner. But he had been young and foolishly believed in the people he loved. That was before he realised that despite giving his love, people either left him behind or betrayed him.

They were drawing closer to their destination. Ace slowed the car and took another peek in the rear-view mirror. The eyes that reflected back at him were dark like a stormy ocean and as unfathomable as an ingrained sapphire wedged within the earth. Even he didn't recognise them. His vision dropped to the handbrake as he yanked it into place. He peered at his swollen hands. They appeared red and indignant and they ached. He sighed and felt the tear in his heart widen at the prospect of what he was about to do. However, he knew there was no other way; he *knew* no other way as he was a stranger to himself.

Some of the hurts you have cured
And the sharpest you still have survived
But what the torments of grief you endured
For evils which never arrived.
—Emerson

Chapter Eleven

ILLIE STOOD BACK TO SURVEY THE FINISHING touches she had applied to her cherub piece. The long tresses of her ponytail bounced down her back as she nodded her approval. The blending worked well and the carnation of her little cherub appeared perfect, creating just the right pigmentation she wanted. She glanced to the over-sized iron clock that hung on the wall in the far side of the studio. 'Crap,' she muttered, scooping up her brushes and plopping them in a jar of turpentine to soak. It was just about time to collect Arella from school, after which she would go home to prepare her special dinner. Well, as special as it got with her culinary skills.

She threw on her cardigan and gathered her bag, rummaging through her belongings for her car keys and sunglasses as she closed the studio door and hurried to the gallery. She spotted Holly at the counter and made a bee-line towards her to plant a kiss on her cheek.

'Got to run! See you tomorrow,' she said breathlessly.

Holly gave her an amused look. 'Annabella's sculptures are just exquisite, don't you agree?' she said.

Millie continued to head for the door. 'Absolutely,' she called back. She paused briefly as the phone started ringing, and glanced at Holly as she reached to open the door.

Holly motioned for her to stop. 'Just a moment,' she uttered to the caller, then looked at Millie. 'It's your father.'

She hesitated with a frown. 'Tell him I'll call him later,' she waved.

Holly nodded and turned back to the phone.

Millie pondered her father's call as she drove the short distance to the school. She hadn't spoken to him for a while, and she knew the time was coming for her to talk things through with him. Yet, she was reluctant to rehash old hurts and past actions. She pulled up in front of the school, and when she began to walk towards the gates where Arella usually met her, she became aware of the light breeze that fluttered through the trees and frolicked against her cheeks in a gentle caress. Pushing aside thoughts of her father, she gazed up towards the trees and watched the quivering leaves with fleeting fascination. She grinned with gratitude at the Australian Gum for keeping its leaves all year round.

The sound of the bell signified the end of the school day, and it wasn't long before children began filing out of their classrooms and boisterously running for the gates. Millie's eyes lit up as she watched them. She always found the animated imagination of children enchanting. She considered it a gift that was all too lost as adulthood loomed, which in most cases caused creative insight to dull. *And that was a tragedy indeed*, she thought.

A few minutes passed and still no Arella. *She's probably chewing her new teacher's ear off*, Millie frowned. Arella had been moved up a grade a few weeks before. She loved her new classroom and her new teacher, Mrs Brooks, speaking often about how she loved to talk to her teacher about the new equations she was learning. Millie fiddled with her keys and suppressed an irritated sigh.

With the parade of children dwindling, her frown deepened as she searched around one last time before deciding to go to Arella's classroom. The gentle breeze suddenly chilled her bones, and she pulled her cardigan around her as her walk became a brisk march. When she reached Arella's classroom, she peeked through the open doorway expecting to find her daughter in deep discussion with the teacher. But when she scanned the room and realised no-one was there, her heart skipped a beat as anxiety crept in. *Where is she?*

Pivoting on her feet, Millie almost stumbled as she rushed to the school office. Her eyes darted, desperate to catch a glimpse of her daughter. By the time she reached the office, she was panting heavily and it took a couple of goes before she could speak in an audible manner.

'I'm looking for my daughter; she didn't come and meet me at the gates. Arella Anderson – is she here?' she gulped.

The woman behind the desk asked who Arella's teacher was and to wait a moment. Millie rolled her eyes and tapped her short nails on the counter top as the woman walked down the hall. She returned a minute later accompanied by another woman who Millie assumed was Arella's teacher. She was dressed in a conservative office pants outfit with chunky gold bangles decorating both her wrists.

'Arella left with all the other kids at bell time; she didn't meet you?' she frowned.

'No, did you see which way she went?' Millie fought the panic in her chest.

Mrs Brooks shook her short blonde hair. 'I'm sorry, I was still at my desk when they all left.'

Millie bit her lip. It wasn't like Arella to just wander off. She would have come to the gates as usual. *She would never leave with a stranger.*

'May I use your phone?' Millie was already walking towards the phone on the other side of the counter.

Mrs Brooks' dark eyes radiated kindness. 'Of course. I'll get a few teachers together and search the school,' she said, turning to hurry deeper into the office.

Millie nodded as her trembling fingers punched in the numbers. *Hurry up, answer the phone!* she thought, listening to the drilling ring in her ear.

'Hello?' Glen answered.

Finally.

'Dad! Is Arella with you?' she quaked.

'No, why? Where is she?' he said.

She squeezed her eyes shut, her throat grew dry. 'I don't know; she didn't meet me at the gate after school. Where could she be?' she quivered.

A noisy gasp reverberated through the phone. 'Oh shit, Millie. I called you earlier … I didn't know; he told me he was good now and fighting off the darkness,' he stammered.

It took a moment for her father's words to soak into her consciousness, and as they fell into her awareness, it felt like a begrudging drip she was unable to stop. She had never hated words more than the ones her father had just uttered. She shook her head and her world began to spin. A sharp pain shot through her head and settled behind her eyes. She slumped against the top of the bench as legs began to feel like jelly.

'Ace. Arella went with Ace?' she whispered.

A chill spiralled through her like a twisting tornado gaining momentum. The colour drained from her face and she felt as if she watched through a pane of glass while the outside world flurried around her. An image of

Ace as she had last seen him flashed through her mind and she shivered as she dropped the phone to the floor.

'Miss Anderson?' the office lady touched her arm.

She jumped and listlessly gazed at her.

'Are you okay? I think we should call the police,' she continued.

Millie nodded. 'Yes,' she murmured.

The woman guided her to a nearby chair and instructed her to sit. Millie collapsed into the chair and buried her face in her hands as deep sobs choked her. 'He has my baby! My little girl.' Her mind cringed and contorted with the jumble of her thoughts, and she felt as if she were suffocating. *Surely, he wouldn't hurt her. Surely.* She remembered how much he had adored Arella, yet when she recalled the fleeting stare of the black serpent with the cold sapphire eyes that night at the retreat, she knew there was no way of telling what he might do.

She shuddered. 'I need to use the phone again,' she mumbled.

There was no time to allow fear to overtake her; she had to clear her mind. She knew he really wanted her, and Arella was the perfect bait.

He was unable to stop the tremble of his hands as he carried the plate over to the table. Glen hated waiting around to hear news of Arella. He felt useless and responsible. *There must be something else I can do?* he fretted. He had already given as much information as he could remember to the police. He had barely glanced at the van Madison had brought back with her after her walk. Just as he was placing his omelette layered plate on the table, he lost his grip and the plate slipped from his hands and shattered to the floor.

'Shit,' he grumbled, surveying the mess. His stomach moaned with disappointment while he contemplated salvaging the remains of his stuffed omelette. Most of it was still intact. *If I just pick out the chunks of plate, it'll be fine*, he reasoned.

He set about scraping the omelette to a new plate and cleaned up the broken dish that had exploded over the floor, then he sat at the table to eat the meal he had prepared. He took a mouthful and nodded to himself. *Yum, it wasn't ruined.* Yet with the next bite of food, the egg became crunchy and gritted loudly against his teeth. He shrugged and continued eating between hefty sips of water.

A knock on the door fractured his otherwise quiet meal. *I hope they've found my Rella!*

He scrambled to the door and threw it opened forcibly, stopping short when his eyes found Lilly.

'Hello Glen,' she said.

Reminding himself to close his jaw, Glen stumbled over his greeting. He stood in the door frame looking as awkward as he felt and finding it extremely difficult to process her presence.

She gave a short smile. 'I hope I'm not interrupting anything important. May I come in?' she said.

He blinked. 'Erm … no … no, I was just eating plate. Come in,' he mumbled.

He led her to the kitchen and motioned for her to take a seat while he stiffly did the same. He noticed her looking about the kitchen with interest. She looked considerably better than the last time he had seen her, but then she had been wounded and at death's door.

Her blue eyes glinted. 'Some things don't change,' she remarked.

His eyes flitted to hers before slipping away. 'And some things do,' he said.

She nodded slightly while reaching for her bag and pulling out a folder. He noted the strands of grey that curled over the hairline of her face, and the lines that crinkled her forehead. Otherwise, her skin appeared fleshy and full; healthy.

He eyed the folder suspiciously as she placed it on the table. 'Are you here about Arella?' he asked.

Her puzzled expression revealed her answer before she spoke. 'No, why would say that?' she replied.

He ignored her question. 'Then why did you come here, Lilly?'

She took a breath. 'I want to marry Scott,' she said.

His eyes fell to the folder again. 'Oh ...' he stammered.

She reached for her bag and drew out a pen. She placed the pen on top of the folder then pushed it closer to him. 'Can you please sign the divorce papers?' her eyes pleaded.

He took the folder and slowly opened it. His eyes trailed over a bunch of typed words with bright little stick-it arrows indicating where his signature should fall. He glanced back at her, noticing the slight quiver of her hands as she knuckled them together.

'Why did you bring them yourself? You could have sent someone else or mailed them?' he said.

She gulped visibly. 'There are many things I would have done differently. Marrying you and raising the children are not on that list,' she sighed, and her eyes glistened. 'It is what came after that I regret; what happened with Ace ... it's my fault,' she choked.

Her eyes dropped to her knotted hands. 'I want to do things differently now; I want to reach out to our son and I want to do things the right way,' she whispered.

He strained against the tears that threatened to overwhelm him. 'For what it's worth, I'm sorry, Lilly,' he said.

'I'm sorry too.' She reached out and patted his hand

briskly. It was the final scrap of affection to symbolise their time together, and it was enough to topple the tears from Glen's eyes as he signed the papers with blurred vision.

He was unable to meet her eyes as his colossal fingers pushed the folder towards her. 'I hope you will be happy with him,' he grunted.

Her smile was thin. 'Thank you,' she uttered.

She replaced the folder in her bag and made moves to leave. They walked the stretch of hallway in silence, then she turned to him as she reached the door. 'Hey, were you really eating plate?' she asked.

He rubbed a hand over the top of his hair. 'Yeah,' he grinned sheepishly.

'I guess some things *do* change. Since when did you become a plate eater?' she laughed.

'Since my omelette and plate decided to unite in a special way,' he chuckled. His eyes grew serious. 'You should go to Millie now. She needs you; you can be there for her in a way she won't allow me.'

She gave a look of alarm. 'What's happened?' she said.

His lips creased together and his eyes darkened. 'Ace happened,' he said painfully.

'Can we stop for something to eat, uncle Ace?' Arella piped over the radio.

Madison cringed and tried to focus her attention on the lights of the oncoming traffic. The widespread beams of the passing headlights caught her eye and she relaxed; she had always enjoyed night driving and she appreciated the trip back north in the comfort of the van. If only she were alone with Ace, it might have even become a romantic trip back home.

Ace shot Arella a grin. 'Sure, Rella, we'll pull over soon okay?' he said.

'I have to pee too,' she said.

Madison suppressed a sigh. Who knew she didn't like children? Certainly not she. She had always assumed she liked the little ankle biters, however she had taken an instant dislike to this one. She reached for her bag and blindly dug through its contents. 'Ah, here it is,' she exclaimed, shoving a lollypop towards Arella. 'I got this for you.'

Arella took the lollypop guardedly. 'Thanks,' she muttered. She turned back to Ace. 'I want real food,' she whined.

'It is real food,' Madison snapped.

Ace scowled and threw her a dirty look.

Madison sighed and turned her attention back to the window. She couldn't wait for this part to be over. Then she and Ace would be free to frolic and play as

Apepsis intended, and together they would accumulate enough influence to effectively reincarnate the serpent god on earth. That was when her black magic skills would come in handy. The thought of eradicating enough angel descendants and using her magic for a much higher purpose excited her beyond belief. After all, she had been training for that moment her whole life, and waiting for someone like Ace for just as long.

She took comfort in knowing her time would soon arrive. Her eyes found the dark spidery figures of the trees looming on the side of the road. The Australian bush was ingrained in her upbringing, as she was raised by parents that had embraced and used the land effectively. From the moment she was born, her parents had instilled their shadowy beliefs in their only child, and raised her within the sacred grounds of a coven where they had taught her the folklore of their tradition. Practising hexes and using the tools of the craft had come naturally. Since she could remember, she was fascinated with the supernatural tales her mother whispered in her ear at night; especially those that wove around their serpent god, Apepsis. It was on her 16th birthday she had chosen her fate when she agreed to pledge her life-force to the serpent god in sacrificial ceremony.

A few minutes later the van slowed and pulled up in a dirt lot beside a highway diner. Madison threw open the door and climbed out with an air of relief. She fumbled to light a cigarette, glad to put a little distance between herself and Arella.

Ace came up beside her. 'I'll take her in and meet you inside,' he said, leaning to plant a kiss on her lips. 'C'mon Rella.' He grasped Arella's hand and they made for the diner.

'What do you want to eat?' he smiled down at her.

'French fries and a chocolate shake!' Arella giggled as she skipped along next to him.

Ace chuckled. 'French fries hey? You know they're actually not French; they originated in Belgium,' he said.

'Yes, I did know that!' she laughed. 'Did you know that eating chocolate was once considered a sin?'

Ace laughed. 'It was during the 16th and 17th centuries,' he said.

Their conversation drifted out of Madison's earshot and she eyed them cagily until they disappeared through the diner door. She didn't trust the little squirt. Firstly, she resented the attention Ace lavished on her. And secondly, *we bundled her into a van and away from her mother and not once has she been afraid*. It just didn't make sense.

She stamped out the cigarette, and smoothing the tight sweater over her fleshy hips, sashayed towards the diner. Whatever the kid's game was, she could play too.

Madison slid along the padded bench of the booth facing them. Their laughter paused as they both looked at her. She pushed aside her escalating grudge and forced a smile when Ace said he had ordered her a burger. She thanked him and looked at Arella. 'So, Arella, how long do you think it will take your mother to come for you?' she said sweetly.

Arella's eyes widened. 'She won't take long. I will meet her in the Golden World,' she said, taking a long slurp of her shake.

'Where is the Golden World?' Madison frowned.

Arella shrugged and munched on her hotdog. 'It's a special place for angels – not for bad witches,' she said.

Madison gasped. 'I'm not a bad witch, who told you that?' she shot Ace an accusing glance.

Ace chuckled. 'Don't look at me; she's a smart little cookie,' he winked. He turned to Arella. 'Madi is not a bad witch, Rella. She's my special friend and she helps me.'

'I know ... she helps you do bad things,' she said.

Madison tossed her frizzy locks. 'You're rather a shit, aren't you sweetie?' she hissed.

Arella gasped. 'That's a naughty word,' she said, covering her mouth with her hand. She blinked at Ace. 'I told you she's a bad witch!'

'I told you she's a bad witch,' Madison mimicked. She leaned across the table. 'Bitch. There's another bad word.'

Arella's eyes almost popped from her head as she

turned to Ace.

'Enough!' Ace barked, glaring at Madison. 'Hurry up and eat; I'm going to the bathroom. Be ready to go when I get back.'

Madison smirked. She watched Arella in silence as they ate alone for a few minutes. *Annoying little brat*, she brooded. Her thoughts turned to her visit at the gallery earlier that day, and her mood suddenly shifted. She hadn't left the gallery empty handed as Millie had assumed. She had in her possession a significant ingredient to a crucially important spell. Her eyes gleamed under the fluorescent lights of the diner as elation surged through her with an exquisite shiver. She had concocted a plan of her own when she had picked up the van from her girlfriend's house after her gallery visit. She smiled as she watched Ace walk briskly towards them. He had no idea that they would be expecting another visitor in a few days; a visitor whose presence would play a pivotal part in gaining momentum in the spell she intended to cast.

She threw the napkin to the table and slid from the booth. 'Hurry up!' she snapped at Arella. She started for Ace, careful to use the full swing of her hips as she met him between rows of empty tables. 'We're ready, baby,' she cooed.

'Good,' he grunted. His eyes glinted and his mood had darkened considerably.

'What's wrong?' she asked.

'There is a cop in the bathroom and he was checking me out. Take Arella to the van before he comes out.'

She grabbed Arella's arm roughly. 'Come on!' she said, ushering her towards the door.

'Ouch! Uncle Ace?' Arella moaned.

Ace gave her a gentle shove. 'Go with Madi. I'll be out in just a minute.'

Madison crammed Arella through the van door. 'Stay here; I'll be right back,' she said, ignoring the girl's protests.

She rushed back to the diner and peered through a grimy window. It was late and the restaurant was empty. From her viewpoint, she couldn't even spy the old man that had been busily cleaning behind the counter earlier. *He must be out back*, she assumed. Scanning the room, her breath caught in her throat when she noticed a big black snake slivering between the diner tables and chairs. The snake was like nothing she had ever seen before; it had to be at least 10ft long and although its body was thick, it was the massive width of its head that struck her the most. She watched with growing anticipation as its elongated body flexed with each movement, giving its black scales a luminous effect as they glimmered under the bright diner lights. She grinned. *Oh, he's beautiful!* she thought, totally mesmerised at his graceful mobility.

From the corner of her eye, Madison noticed

another movement in the room. It was the policeman. Her body stiffened and she crouched down further as the uniformed man paused and cautiously peered around the empty diner. He must have sensed danger, as she noticed his hand lingering close to his belted pistol. He took one noiseless step towards the counter, searching for the man that worked the night shift. It was then she saw Ace speed towards the policeman. The man's eyes widened as he made a yelping sound and grappled for his weapon while Ace leered high and arched over him menacingly. Madison gasped with excitement burning through her dark eyes as Ace cocked his head to one side for a moment. She noticed how strikingly blue his lidless eyes appeared against his black scales.

The man took the fleeting moment to grip the handle of his gun, and as he began to raise the pistol towards the hovering serpent, Ace opened his mouth to reveal an impressive display of white pointed fangs. He sprang into action and swooped down to capture the man's head entirely between his strong jaws. The man's body shuddered violently while his limbs flared and swung wildly in a desperate attempt to free himself. Madison noticed his legs kicking savagely as Ace manoeuvred his long sinuous form and easily began to lift his body from the floor. With one powerful thrust, the serpent lashed the man's head and severed it from his body.

Madison's pulse thundered through her body in a

throbbing race, yet she was unable to tear her eyes from the gruesome scene. Blood spouted from the decapitated body like a scarlet fountain, and when her eyes rested on the man's head that had come to pause not far from the window through which she gazed, she flung her hand up to her lips. She was so drawn to the head that she failed to notice Ace slinking to the far side of the restaurant. And as she watched the freshly amputated head, her heart almost stopped when she saw his eyes blink a few times and his pale lips quivering. She gasped as his wandering eyes finally settled on her briefly before glazing over in an expression of shock; as if the finality of his death had permanently marked his face.

She heard the thud of the diner door and slowly became aware of the heavy fall of footsteps as they neared her. She looked at Ace in confusion as he tugged at her arm and hauled her to her feet.

'Let's go,' he grunted.

She allowed him to bundle her into the van while her thoughts still recalled the man's decapitated head. An hour had passed before she was able to drag herself away from the grisly diner scene. She swallowed and shook her frizzy locks as she looked to him. It was dark but every now and then his silhouette ignited with the light of a passing truck. His chest was heaving under his jacket and he wore a calloused expression. Her nerves tingled with elation. It encircled every channel of her body until settling in her groin. She eyed him with lust and squirmed in her seat as she felt herself becoming moist. Her eyes trailed to Arella who was resting her sleeping head against Ace.

'Hey lover,' she said huskily. 'We need to go off road for a few minutes.'

He glanced at her, and catching her expression, stopped the car. He didn't need much convincing.

Chapter Twelve

MILLIE DIDN'T BOTHER TO KNOCK. SHE FLUNG the door open and slammed it shut again with a kick of her heel. Her footsteps fell heavily on the old timber floorboards, and just as she expected, her father appeared clambering towards her as she skirted the kitchen doorway.

His green eyes were vivid. 'Millie! What's going on? Have you heard any word about Rella?' he exclaimed.

'Are you serious?' her voice was like steel.

'What do mean?' he said.

Her fingers dug into the door frame. 'I just spoke to the police. You told them they were headed south. Why?'

Their eyes locked and for a moment he was silent.

'We both know he was in Queensland, and we both know that's where he's headed with her. Why did you tell the police he was going south?' she said.

Glen nodded slowly. 'I was wondering how long it would take for you to come here.' He lowered his eyes and walked over to the table, gesturing for her to sit down.

'What have you done? Where is she?' she smouldered.

'I don't know where she is exactly, but we won't get her back with the police, Millie. He's too powerful … and the woman that accompanies him is almost as dangerous as him. We have to do this together; it's the only way,' he said.

Her mind whirled. *What woman?*

'Millie, listen to me. I tried to tell you earlier but you wouldn't listen. I had to lead the police the wrong way – at least for now,' he said.

Her lips felt dry as she bit down. 'It's me he wants,' she said gravely.

Glen nodded. 'Yes, but he's conflicted. I know there is still good in him. He won't hurt her; I'm sure of it.'

Millie loosened her grip on the door frame and sank into a chair. Her face pale milk yet the fire that blazed in her eyes betrayed her rage. 'I want to know everything you know about Ace, the woman and where exactly they're going,' she demanded. 'I want to know everything you know about this Apepsis. Everything!'

He drew a heavy breath and rubbed at the spikes of his hair. 'They are headed back north; he wanted us to know that. The serpent seeps through his mind and clogs his consciousness. Years I have struggled to contain his presence, sometimes with success ... and other times I lost the inner battle. I owe my redemption to you; it was your grace that ultimately saw me banish Apepsis for good,' he said.

Noticing his eyes glistening as he spoke, she reached out and covered his hand with her own. 'Go on,' she whispered.

'It has taken me many years to overcome the darkness, but you helped me realise that there is only one true power that can create anything, and when requalified, that energy has the power to consume and recreate. What I'm telling you is; it is the same for Ace – the darkness in him can be recreated into light. He just needs our help.'

Millie paused in thought. 'I'll book us a flight to Queensland. What of the woman?' she said.

His eyes darkened with his scowl. 'She's a black witch, and she belongs to Apepsis,' he said.

She gave a bitter laugh and rose to her feet. 'Well, he can have her, but he's claiming my family no longer.' She walked to the doorway and paused to look at him. 'Damon will be joining us; that is another subject we will discuss some day.'

'Millie, I'm sorry for everything ... I really am,' he choked.

Her expression softened. 'I know, dad. I know,' she murmured.

She turned and made a swift exit. As the chill of the outside air blasted into her lungs, she felt a moment of gratitude. For the first time since she had discovered the secrets she had uncovered in that wooden box years before, she was finally able to release the resentment she had harboured for her father. He had found his peace, and she realised when they left this earth; the lies, the betrayal and the tension would become irrelevant. All that mattered now was getting her daughter back and saving her lost brother.

She drove the short distance home to make the arrangements for their trip north. Later she intended to seek divine guidance from Samantha. She knew she had to expand enough to reach the Golden World; for there she would contact her daughter.

The hospital corridors were quiet. Bella shuddered as she delved deeper into the building. The walls were washed with grey and appeared as dull and lifeless as the patients that occupied the beds. *They could at least attempt to make it a happier atmosphere*, she thought. She rounded the last corner that would bring her to her mother's room, and clutched the yellow carnations tighter when she saw her. Her mother was lying as still as the dead, and for a moment Bella was unsure if life remained within her. As she moved closer, she sighed with relief when her mother's eyes fluttered open.

'Hi mum,' she whispered, leaning over to kiss her forehead.

Rose smiled. 'Hi Wonder-Bella,' she murmured. She chuckled quietly. 'I've been waiting for you.'

Bella busied herself with arranging the fresh flowers in a vase. 'I'm sorry; I got held up at work. There were lots of swimming lessons tonight.' She perched on the edge of the bed.

Rose reached for Bella's hand; her faded eyes twinkled. 'Tell me, did Mr Adams call in to see you Saturday night?'

Bella frowned in mockery. 'You know he did.'

She gave her hand a gentle squeeze. It felt bony and frail in her hold, she suppressed the concern that threatened to break her expression. 'I have to tell you something important. Remember when daddy would say I was a gift from the angels to the world?'

Rose nodded. 'Yes.'

Bella leaned in and lowered her voice. 'I found out today that I have wings,' she whispered.

She searched for an expression of disbelief but it didn't come.

A low chuckle escaped her mother lips as she reached to stroke Bella's hair. 'Now you know your true heritage and you're aware that death is only a transition from one plane to the next. Now I can leave in peace, because you *know* you are not alone.'

Bella gasped. 'What do you mean, my true heritage?'

Rose turned to the set of drawers near her bed and made slight rasping noises as she rummaged through the top one. She revealed an envelope. 'Everything you need to know is written here. Don't grieve my death, Bella. I will not be far from your reach,' she said.

Bella shut her eyes and filled her lungs with the thick stale odour that lingered between the walls while her whole being was overcome with a combination of love and foreboding. She opened her eyes again and re-garded her mother. She knew it was time to let her go.

'I love you,' she croaked.

'I love you too,' Rose murmured.

Their hands interlaced as Rose closed her eyes. Her pale lips smoothed in a serene crease before her facial muscles relaxed and slanted in the final downslide as her energy left her body. Bella felt her mother's hands go limp. She caught the sob in her throat as a silent flood of tears cascaded down her face. She rested her head against her mother's motionless chest. 'I love you, I love you, I love you,' she whispered.

Bella envisioned her mother reuniting with her fa-ther. They stood by the glittering sapphire waters of the

Golden World and appeared youthful and joyous. They smiled and waved farewell before they meshed together as one brilliant thread of light, then disappeared from her mind's eye. Her heart swelled with love and gratitude, and although her mother's death saddened her, she had found a place of acceptance within her soul. She knew they were not gone from her existence; only from the physical plane in which she remained.

When Bella later left the hospital, she was surprised to feel a shift take place within her. Knowing her mother was no longer trapped in the web of illness, lifted her spirit; especially since she had perceived her parents' reunion. She drove home in a strange state of nostalgia as she revisited her childhood. Years of treasured moments flashed through her memory in a sweet visionary display.

She turned into her driveway to see a dark figure sitting on the porch steps. As the headlights beamed across the house, she realised it was Craig.

He smiled as she approached. 'Hi,' she said.

'Hi,' he replied.

She sat down next to him and peered into the inky street. The chill of the air turned her breath into visible puffs of mist that mingled with the night. Her eyes dropped to her boots. 'My mother passed away tonight,' she said.

He wrapped a hand around hers and curled his

fingers around her knuckles. 'I'm sorry,' he murmured.

She bent her head to rest against his shoulder. His sweet spicy aroma gave her a sense of comfort. 'Everything changes; even when nothing new happens, it's still changing. We just have to learn how to cope with the transitions,' she said.

He reached into his satchel bag. 'Will chocolate help with this transition?' he offered.

She grinned and gazed up at him. 'Definitely.'

'Millie always said the same about change. She says that is why we have the power to determine our lives; by using our thoughts and imaginations,' he said, putting emphasis on the last of his words.

'Makes sense. You two are close, aren't you?' she said.

'She has the uncanny ability to lift my spirits. I have never known anyone like her; until now.' His eyes drifted across to hers. 'I don't mean to say you are like Millie … you are very different, but you both possess a similar gift. I can't explain it, but I can feel it.'

She chuckled as she thought about her encounter with Millie in the studio. 'I think I know what you mean.' She tugged at his hand. 'Come on, let's go inside.'

Once inside, Bella placed her mother's letter on the kitchen table for later. She preferred to read her mother's final words when she was alone, but for now she was grateful for Craig's presence. She put the kettle on and

pulled out two mugs.

'Are you okay?' Craig came up behind her and wrapped her up in his arms

She leaned back into him, revelling in his strong, warm arms. 'I am actually,' she replied.

He gave her a squeeze. 'Did you go to the gallery today?'

'Yes, why?' she said. *Odd question at a time like this.*

His expression grew grim. 'Because Arella was kidnapped this afternoon.'

She pivoted on her feet. 'What? What happened? Who would do such a thing?'

'Millie's brother.'

They sipped steaming mugs of tea and nibbled dark chocolate as Craig filled her in on Arella's disappearance. He threw in a brief family history so she might better understand the circumstances.

'Oh … that's who Millie was talking about today,' she said almost to herself, recalling their earlier conversation about the serpent immersing himself into humans.

Craig frowned. 'Huh?'

'Never mind. What's she going to do?'

His frown deepened. 'She's going there herself,' he said.

She gasped. 'Is that a good idea?'

'I don't know. She's convinced she's the only one

that can help Ace.'

Their conversation stilted as Bella's mind was a whirlpool. *Maybe she needs my help.* She thought again about the sphere of light that appeared over their joined hands, and the wings that had materialised. *I should call her.* Craig was watching her intently and the expression in his eyes revealed a depth of passion that struck through her awareness with a flutter.

'What?' she murmured.

He smoothed back a lock of blonde hair that had fallen over her face. 'What are you thinking?' his voice was raw.

His touch sent ripples down her spine and she fought to keep her breath even. 'I'm wondering how I can help Millie.'

His fingers lingered over her face while his eyes seeped into hers like a melting pot of honey. Her breath quickened with his feathery touch that traced promises against her skin. She had wanted to burn for him from the first day they met, and every inch of her yearned for him to fan her blaze. Her eyes trailed to his lips. They were plump and fleshy as they parted to speak, but she stopped him with a fast clinging kiss.

Their mouths crushed and united with a hint of desperation while their hands snaked and tangled in each other's hair. His breathing became short and raspy between deep explorations that heightened the arousal that scattered through her body. He trailed his warm hands under her thick sweater and found the small hooks of her bra. His probing tongue paused briefly when he unclasped the bra and freed her aching breasts.

Bella drew back from him, panting. She looked at him through hungry eyes and her head swam with headiness as she removed her sweater and discarded the bra. His eyes stayed on her as she rolled down her stockings and panties, and threw them aside. The kitchen light skimmed over the curves of her pale body. She felt the colour flush over her cheeks and she bit down on her lip as she stood before him wearing only a red tartan skirt. His smile reassured her as she stepped closer with a purposeful sway to her hips.

She paused. He swallowed hard and squirmed slightly on the chair while her eyes dropped to his parted legs and her mouth loosened at the sight of the swell beneath his jeans.

He grabbed her hand and pulled her towards him. 'You're so beautiful,' he said.

She sank to her knees, and when their eyes locked, she was overwhelmed as her emotions shifted into overdrive. 'So are you,' she purred.

He snatched her up, capturing her lips and violating her mouth with his own while kneading her breasts like dough. Her moan was swallowed with their kiss, and a sense of urgency billowed through her as she became aware of her moist yearning.

When she straddled him, he gripped her thighs and entered her. A pleasurable cry escaped her lips while her hips moved like a steam engine surging down the tracks to meet its destination. Her head spun in a dizzy pitch as her craving reached a peak and her cries reverberated in a low groan.

Afterwards, Bella made fresh tea while he scooped up the remaining chocolate and they trekked upstairs to her bedroom. She watched him while he slowly sucked at a piece of dark chocolate.

'I love the way the layers just melt in your mouth,' she said.

He popped a piece in his mouth. 'Especially after a sip of hot tea,' he said.

'I'm hearing ya!' she laughed.

She placed her mug on the bedside table and fell into his outstretched arms. They snuggled down into the bed with their limbs intertwining. Soon, she drifted into a deep slumber.

A little girl's voice called softly. Bella turned towards the sound as it reached her ears again and found her vision captivated with the green rolling hills. The sun's lowering rays filtered through clouds and cast a golden streak over the plunging valleys.

'Bella,' the voice called again.

Bella gazed at the clouds. They were full and vivid and they reminded her of sugary pillows of cotton candy. She stepped into a streaming light and started her ascension. The sun burned bright, yet as she drew closer, she felt no heat. She welcomed the sense of tranquillity that encompassed her, and accepted the blissful path into the Golden World.

'Bella!' Arella waved franticly. She was standing between the lofty arches of the unicorn gates, and leaped into her arms as Bella drew near.

Bella laughed. 'Arella, what are you doing here?' She regarded the gates with a slight frown. 'I've never seen these before.'

'It's my creation,' Arella beamed. 'Do you like them?'

'Oh, nice touch; they're breathtaking.'

Arella gently tugged at her hand. Her little face scrunched as she became serious. 'We don't have much time, we are almost there.'

'Almost where, honey?' Bella said.

'I'm with my uncle Ace and his girlfriend, Madison. She's a witch and not so nice at all! We are driving in a white van ... and I heard them speak of the Mary Valley. I've been waiting here for mummy, but she hasn't found the way here yet. Can you tell her?' she spluttered.

Bella watched Arella with fascination. Her aquamarine eyes appeared dynamic and striking as they mutated between blue and green as she spoke; it was hypnotic. Then it dawned on her as she remembered the events surrounding Arella. She reached to cup Arella's chin. 'Of course, I'll tell her. Are you safe?'

Arella's dark hair jiggled over her shoulders. 'My uncle won't hurt me … and he won't let her hurt me either.' She threw her arms around Bella's neck. 'I think he's hurt other people though. Tell my mummy to be careful!' she whispered.

'I promise I will,' Bella said.

'Oh, we're here! They're trying to wake me! I have to go!' Arella stammered as her image faded in a slow dissolve.

Bella froze. She looked at the unicorn gates, her thoughts weaving in cluttered threads. Never had she communicated with someone from her world in this celestial place, and it was taking a few turns of her mind to adjust to Arella's appearance; *and her disappearance.* Her thoughts began to untangle as she realised the significance of this meeting. She burned the arching gates into her memory as she intentionally willed herself to awaken.

Bella woke with a start. Her eyes widened instantly as unicorns danced through her mind. *Arella!* She pried herself from under Craig's arm and quietly padded downstairs to the kitchen. She hit the button on the kettle while she tried to gather her thoughts. *It's way too early to call Millie yet. She might think me crazy! Hmmm*, she pondered, pulling out a mug and ladling it with sugar. Somehow, she knew Millie wouldn't think she was going mad. Her eyes fell to her mother's letter. She finished making her tea, then settled at the table to read the letter.

'*Dear Annabella …*

Chapter Thirteen

I T WAS EARLY. DEW CLUNG HEAVILY TO EACH BLADE of grass and shone under the rising sun. Ace filled his lungs with the pledging fresh scent of a new day. He scanned the low mist that shrouded the waters of the river below. He could hear the rush of the river as it vigorously cascaded over rock edges, yet he could only discern the slight watery sprays from their constant conflict. He stood on the edge of a giant sandstone ledge overlooking the gorge. He could see fertile flats that gave way to rolling green pastures, and the lifeblood of the Mary Valley as the river cut and snaked its way towards the Great Sandy Strait.

Ace had discovered this place when bushwalking not long after he had arrived at the valley the year before. He had instantly felt drawn to the magnificent view of the gorge below, and he liked the solitary feel of the boulder clearing. He had often come here to make the shift. The gorge and the precarious position of the rock reminded him of his insignificance, and he had often

almost slipped to his death; he had even contemplated taking that final step. But not this day. He assumed the final yoga pose of the session and gazed at the warming sun. Arella should be due to awaken soon, and he couldn't wait to show her his special place. He pulled the hoodie low over his head and started his jog back to the cabin. He enjoyed having his niece with him. Much more than he had anticipated.

'What is this?' Arella screwed up her nose at the a jar she held between her fingertips.

Madison snatched it from her. 'Never *you* mind, young lady,' she snapped.

Arella's mouth curled at the edges. 'But it looks like toad legs. Ewww!'

She spotted another jar and her face almost exploded with bewilderment. 'Ooo ... that's disgusting! What is in *that* jar? It looks like shrivelled up soggy ping-pong balls!'

Madison rolled her eyes. 'Just go and eat your breakfast.'

'How am I supposed to eat after seeing this stuff?' Arella retorted.

Madison nudged her towards the kitchen. 'Well,

how about you don't look at it?'

Arella dragged her feet to the kitchen and sat at the small round table. 'Too late,' she said.

Ace slammed through the door and gaped at them. 'What's going on here? I can hear you two bickering from outside,' he said.

'Are all kids this annoying?' Madison switched on the stereo and turned the knob while giving Arella a spiteful stare.

Natalie Imbruglia's *Torn* filled the small cottage at high volume, and she began to sing along at the top of her voice.

Ace scowled and muttered under his breath as he turned down the sound. The burn of his frown charred Madison. 'You are behaving like a child,' he growled.

Madison flinched, then shrugged and made for the door. 'Whatever; I'm going to take a shower,' she muttered.

He grunted then turned to Arella with a smile.

'She's got jars full of all kinds of gross things!' Her eyes widened accusingly. 'It's not normal Uncle Ace; I told you she is a witch.'

He sat next to her and ruffled her hair. 'Hey, do you see any black cats around here?' he joked.

'Nope, but that doesn't mean a thing,' she said.

'Why is that?' he fought to hide his grin.

'Because, if a witch becomes human, her black cat

will no longer live in her house,' she said crisply.

'Oh, I'm impressed with your witch knowledge,' he chuckled. 'But you don't need to worry about her, okay. She just has to get used to having you around, that's all.'

Her face dropped to the cereal bowl on the table. She picked up her spoon with a short sigh and began to poke around her food.

'Hey, what's up buttercup?' he pried.

'I miss my mummy,' she said.

'I know. She will be here soon,' he said.

She stared into her food. 'I know what you're trying to do, but it won't work because you still love her.'

He leaned closer to her. 'What do you know about love? You still see the world in colours as I once did.' He brushed back a lock of her hair. 'One day you'll learn love only leads to tragedy and disappointment.'

A scorching pain shot through his head and he rubbed at his temples with his fingers. He glanced at her and could see she was struggling not to cry. She looked as if she were suspended between a place of uncertainties and all-knowing; she appeared lost and found all at the same time. The bitter shell that fringed his heart lurched as his resolve cracked around the edges. He realised he hadn't considered Arella's feelings when he had concoct-ed his plans. A moment of regret shuddered through him.

Arella gazed up at him and blinked. 'But I love you

and my heart doesn't feel tragic or disappointed.'

'Finish your breakfast, I want to show you a special place; my secret place. Wanna check it out?' he offered.

She smiled blandly. 'Sure, uncle Ace,' she said.

'Great! Let me go change and we'll head off.' He abruptly rose from the table.

A wave of relief flooded through him when he turned his back on her. He could barely look at her without guilt creeping in. *No, don't be a soft-cock!* he cursed inwardly. His mind shifted to the greater plan and he welcomed the next stab of pain as it daggered through his head. He reached the bedroom and leaned against the door while shutting his eyes. He took a breath as he allowed the internal struggle to drain from his mind. Long ago he had learned to block out the feelings that had only served to weaken him, and the shift towards the frigid chill of the black serpent came all too easily; *His* poisonous fangs proved too powerful for him to fight, even if he desired. Riches and power awaited with the elimination of the Ascended Angels. *Now that's worth striving for,* he reminded himself as he thought about Millie's wings. *Besides, she betrayed me.*

His psyche dulled as hatred fuelled the deepest recesses of his mind and his world turn pitch-black. He craved the sweet taste of revenge. *This was no time to become weak.* He pulled on some fresh clothes and reached for the door with renewed determination. *These are vital*

times; a time when rivals finally play out the end game.
And he was always one for end games.

'Oh, thank God,' Madison muttered when she heard
the cottage door shut as Ace and Arella left. She was
still holed up in the tiny bathroom after deliberately
prolonging her shower. She wiped at the foggy mirror
and peered at herself. Her eyes were rimmed with the
distinct mark of shadows and her freckled features appeared bright against her pale, freshly scrubbed skin.
She poked out her tongue at her reflection and screwed
up her face. *Even my tongue is fat and ugly*, she thought.
Her dark eyes bladed as she assessed herself with loathing. She had never liked the way she looked. No matter how hard she scrubbed, she could never wash away
the dirty feeling inside that stuck with her like a second
skin. She figured that was the reason she had gravitated
so freely towards Apepsis and the ways of black magic.
If she had been a beauty, perhaps she would have at-
tracted the lovelier things in life. Perhaps she would feel
purer within.

Her thoughts drifted towards the imminent arrival of her friend later that day. Madison never understood why her friend was drawn to the dark path, as

her beauty was radiant; even at the blackest of times. They had been raised within the same coven and grew up as blood sisters. *Blood sisters,* she mused. She vividly recalled her blonde friend smeared with goat's blood the night they both had pledged themselves to Apepsis. Her turquoise eyes had glinted lucidly against the flames of the fire and her features were frozen in torment; yet even then her beauty had been unmistakable.

Madison had often dreamed of taking her blood sister for herself. *She* was her only frailty. Yet it was a weakness that was worth the wait. A tingle of longing shimmied down her spine at the thought of seeing her again so soon. Her presence was vital in the hex they planned; two witches were more powerful than one. *But perhaps her presence may serve me in other integral areas too,* she mused. Her friend always had a soft spot for men like Ace; even more so when she would learn of his powers.

Her lips moved as she began to hum a tune and reach for her make-up. 'Today we shall conjure your beauty with paint!' she remarked to her reflection. A smile permeated her face. 'And then we shall conjure up all hell.'

Oh, to be the darkest of black witches!

The sun hung low to the west of the mountains, and the air was becoming damp when Ace and Arella returned to the cottage. The first stars of the evening appeared against the deepening horizon.

Arella grasped Ace's hand. 'Wait! Look!' she said, pointing towards the stars. 'The first stars of the night!'

'Over there is the planet Venus, and some nights Jupiter can be spotted that way, Mars sits somewhere in this direction,' Ace said, pointing at the sky.

Her brows furrowed. 'Wait, how do you know that?' she asked.

He shrugged. 'I've been fascinated with the stars since I was a child … since I really took notice of them.'

'I can see why. They remind us of expansion,' she said.

He chuckled. 'C'mon, let's expand inside. I have to go out for a while, but I'll be back soon.'

She halted. 'You mean you're leaving me alone with her?'

'Not for too long. I have to go see a guy; he called earlier this morning.' He opened the cottage door.

'Seriously?' she griped.

'Yeah,' he said.

His curiosity was piqued when Madison had told him Warren sounded grim when he had called that morning while he was out.

Ace's thoughts were interrupted when he spotted a tall blonde standing at Madison's altar. She was inspecting

Madison's jar collection and arranging various ingredients around the cauldron. Her long hair hung loosely down her back and flipped elegantly when she turned to face them.

She dazzled them with a smile. 'Well, hello. You must be Ace,' she said. Her hips swayed as she sashayed towards them.

His eyes fell to her stilettos and traced up the longest legs he thought he had ever seen before settling on her face. His nose flared at her sweet scent and he scraped his teeth lightly with the tip of his tongue. *Things just got a little more interesting around here.*

'You may be a little over-dressed for this country,' he chuckled.

Her long lashes fluttered. 'My mother always told me to dress like it's the best day of my life.'

'Well, it just may be the best day of your life, sug-ar-puss' he winked.

Her smile was all sauce. 'From what Madi tells me, I'm pretty sure we may get close,' she said.

'Oh, aren't you just the perfect little vixen!' he responded.

They grinned at each other while a current of desire flowed between their eyes.

Madison appeared from the back of the cottage, stopping short when she noticed Ace and Arella. She was quick to reach his side, almost knocking Arella over as she snaked her arms around him. She nuzzled at his ear and pulled at his lobe with her teeth before throwing her friend a triumphant look.

'Baby, we have a visitor,' she said.

He hadn't taken his eyes from her. 'And does our visitor have a name? Or should I just call her vixen?'

'You can call me whatever you like, baby. Or you can just call me Selina,' she laughed.

He licked his lips. 'Well, hello Selina.'

Arella rolled her eyes. 'Yeah hello, I'm here too!' She waved up at the adults.

Selina smiled down at her. 'Hello there little girl,' she said before looking back at Madison. 'I'm going to keep prepping for tonight.'

She spun around with a flick of her hair and sauntered back to the altar.

Madison grabbed Ace's hand and led him to the kitchen. 'I'm sorry I didn't know,' she said.

He thrust her against the counter and kissed her roughly. She opened her mouth around his and franticly pushed up against him. He gripped at her hair and seized her head as he pulled away from her. The blue of his eyes darkened as they penetrated hers.

'I don't like surprises,' he growled.

'I know, I know,' she whispered.

He tightened his hold on her scalp. She winced and a small shriek escaped her lips. 'Who is she and what is she doing here?' he hissed.

She flinched. 'She's my blood sister. She's come for the van; I burrowed it from her! Besides, we have to practise a ritual tonight; for Apepsis. Please, you're hurting me,' she said.

His jaw hardened. 'What ritual?' he demanded.

'The binding of evil sorcerers. We perform the ritual with each season. It's vital for the rise of Apepsis. Ace, please,' she pleaded.

'It's a spell for the conjuration of Apepsis, Ace,' Selina's voice sliced between them.

Ace whirled around to look at her. She was casually leaning on the door frame toying with a small glass dripper bottle. He loosened his hold on Madison.

'Apepsis is *your* serpent god, no?' Selina said.

He nodded.

'Then it's best you let us get on with our witchery. We do need a little privacy though,' she said.

He looked from one to the other. 'I'm going over to Warren's for a few hours. You wait until Rella is sleeping before you start,' he said gruffly. His lips curled as he focused on Madison. 'Do you understand? You wait for her to go to sleep.'

'Yes, of course. Thank you, baby,' she said.

He strolled to the door, pausing in front of Selina. He looked her over before reaching for her breasts. His beefy fingers easily found what he was looking for over the sheer

fabric of her blouse. He took an erect nipple between his fingers and clamped down hard.

'When I return we perform my kind of ritual,' he jeered, rolling her flesh firmly.

Selina's eyes flashed. 'We will be ready,' she promised.

He gave a low grunt, then stalked from the kitchen. 'Fucking witches,' he muttered.

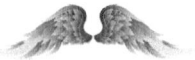

Damon was hunched over an image of a map. 'So where do you want to start searching tomorrow?'

The three of them had barely stopped since arriving in Brisbane earlier that morning. After hiring a car, their vigorous search for Arella had begun by scouring through the Brisbane hinterland and national parks, but they had soon realised it was like trying to find a needle in a haystack.

Millie pinched the bridge of her nose and closed her eyes while she thought. 'Okay, we need to think more rural. Dad said he was working farms,' she said.

'But there's a thousand farms up here! We need to tell the police, Millie,' he frowned.

The volume of the TV increased in the background. She grimaced at Glen. 'Just give me one more day, please,' she said.

She took Damon's hands. 'I know what he is, and he knows what I am. I need to try and get to him before the police; it's the only way I can help my brother.'

Damon gritted his teeth. 'What do you mean who you are? Brother or not, he's taken our daughter. One more day, Millie; that's it,' he said.

'Look at this!' Glen called over his shoulder. He pointed to the TV. 'A policeman was murdered at a town near Coffs Harbour; it's him. I know it,' he said.

Millie and Damon watched the news story in grim silence.

Damon's brow furrowed. 'They're saying there were no witnesses and the man's injuries are likely to be caused by some kind of animal,' he said.

'They're calling for the couple last seen in the diner before the attack to come forward,' Millie said. Her eyebrows raised. 'A couple with a little girl.'

Damon scratched his head. 'That guy was decapitated. I haven't seen your brother in years; but how is it he could tear a man's head off like an animal?' His voice trembled.

Millie and Glen stared at each other. Glen gave her a nod and she sighed heavily. 'Damon, I think you better sit down,' she murmured.

Millie flicked her fingers under the shower water and adjusted the temperature before stepping into the recess and totally immersing herself under the firm spray. She felt her tension subside as the warm water saturated her body. She shut her eyes and pushed aside whirling thoughts, deliberately focusing her attention on the water as it cascaded over her body. She became aware of every drop of water as it sprinkled over her, and with every micro collision, she felt its energising properties renewing the cells of her body.

Her thoughts turned to Damon. He had taken their revelations surprisingly well. *As well as could be expected when you discover half of your girlfriend's family are infected with serpent-like gifts*, she mused. And that *she* possessed a gift of her own. That, he seemed to accept without question; almost. The disbelief on his face was obvious at the revelation that Ace could change form and she could somehow grow a set of wings. Still, she did notice him warming up to the idea as she answered some of his queries.

'Just because you don't believe in something, doesn't make it less true,' she had said.

Damon had smiled awkwardly. 'I need to get some air, Millie-pie.'

She knew it was a lot for him to consider. Yet at a time like this, she didn't have the luxury of easing him into the reality of her family's special abilities. It was just as well she had known him since childhood.

She heard the loud shrill of the phone over the running shower before her father's heavy footsteps and thud at the bathroom door.

'Millie! Millie! You have to come to the phone!' he bellowed.

She wrapped a towel around her and hurried out. 'Yes?' she panted into the phone while making a small puddle at her feet.

'Millie, thank God! I have been trying to track you down. You left so early this morning and I missed you,' Bella stammered.

'What is it, Bella? Has something happened?' she asked.

Bella's voice became urgent. 'Yes; I spoke to Arella last night. I know where she is!' she said.

'What do you mean you spoke with her?' Where?' Millie replied.

'The Golden World,' Bella said hesitantly.

'The Golden World? I've been trying to connect with her there, but I think I've been trying too hard,' Millie whispered. She felt a slight tingle start around the wet strands of her hair and travel over her neck like a gentle breeze. She squeezed her eyes together. *Oh, thank God for Bella!*

'Mary Valley. She's somewhere in the Mary Valley. Millie, there's something else. I'm flying up tonight to

help,' Bella said.

'Bella, my brother is deadly. I don't want to involve you, it's too dangerous.'

'No, you don't understand – I'm coming!' Bella insisted.

She was about to argue the point further when the line went dead. She pulled the handset from her ear and looked at it accusingly. 'Great,' she muttered, turning to look at Glen. 'I guess I know where to start looking tomorrow.' She started back towards the bathroom.

'How did she know?' Glen said.

She chuckled. 'Bella reached out to her in another realm. Wait till I explain this one to Damon,' she said.

Chapter Fourteen

ARELLA TOSSED AN ARM OVER HER FACE. A glower painted her features while she encountered a fretful sleep. She groaned softly and her eyes fluttered open. A feeling of dread overwhelmed her. *Something isn't right.* Her eyes widened at the sound of the grim chant that found her ears. She turned her head on the pillow and faced the closed bedroom door. She could discern a sliver of light from the gap between the bottom of the door and the floor, yet all seemed quiet inside the cottage.

A high-pitched wail flowed through the window. Arella gasped and sunk further under the sheets, scrunching the blankets over her face. The intonations continued like an out-of-tune melody, and as she listened closer, she recognised one of the voices. *It's Madison!* She peeped through a small crack in the blankets towards the window. Her jaw clamped shut and her nostrils flared when she noticed the curtains appeared to glow like a slow-moving sunset behind a mountain. She drew back

the blankets and silently tip-toed to the window. Her muscles tensed and her pulse raced as she reached up to pull the curtain aside.

Her mouth became dry and Arella could barely swallow when she saw a framed circle of wildfire. The flames licked over the grass with vigour, casting eerie shadows into the bordering bushland. Her breath caught in her throat when she noticed two dark figures moving in the circle. They were dressed identically in flowing black gowns and appeared to float as they swayed together. As her eyes adjusted, she saw their faces were smeared with a dark ink-like substance.

Madison and Selina's chanting quietened as they turned their attention to the cauldron in the centre of the flamed circle. It was perched above its own little fire and they were adding ingredients as they murmured to one another. Suddenly, a loud bell sounded over the low crackle of flames. Arella's eyes bulged when she spied a large knife in Selina's hands. Madison surrendered her wrist to the blade and allowed her blood to drip freely into the cauldron. The bell rang again as Selina did the same, allowing her blood to fall into the mix.

A small cry echoed in Arella's ears. She scanned the dark yard in search of the little cries. The bellows grew and reached a hysterical peak. It was then she noticed Madison was holding a tiny lamb in her arms. Her heart constricted and her eyes stung with the salt of her tears as she watched as Selina slit the lamb's throat with a swift flick of the knife.

Arella squeezed her eyes shut. Her chest heaved with the images that burned into her mind. Her head began to spin and giddiness crept over her. She tried to steady herself against the window frame as she felt her legs buckle under her weight. She grasped at the curtains and turned her eyes to the bed. *It's not that far, only a few steps. I can make it.* She released the curtain and took a step. As she felt herself tumbling to the floor, an involuntary cry reverberated through the cottage. She gazed to the curtains listlessly. *I love falling sunsets over the mountains*, she thought. Then her world turned black.

Madison leaned against the kitchen benchtop while taking a long sip of red wine and grinned. She revelled in the euphoric high that followed their rituals. Her gaze settled on Selina.

Selina smiled back and pushed back crimson-tinted blonde hair from her face. 'Great ritual. Apepsis is pleased; I can feel his zeal,' she said.

Madison agreed. She too could feel his pleasing presence; a sure confirmation their sacrificial ritual had been a success.

'Poor Ace. He will miss out on the sibling confrontation he so yearns for,' she laughed, thinking of the piece of hair she had been able to steal from Millie during her gallery visit. This allowed them to combine their conjuration spell with a powerful evil hex which was certain to bring discord and darkness to Millie.

'It's for the greater good. With his sister out of the way, he'll be free to focus on less personal matters,' Selina said.

Madison glanced to the witch-head clock mounted on the kitchen wall. 'Speaking of which, he's due back soon. We better go wash up; the night is far from over,' she winked as she looked Selina over suggestively. *And I can't wait!* she thought, turning to head for the bathroom.

She stopped short and all desire dissolved into irritation when she saw Arella standing beside the kitchen door. 'What are you doing up?' she snapped.

Arella watched them silently. Her eyes were as wide as a doe-eyed cow, yet there was a radiant current moving through them. Madison's frown deepened as she attempted to push aside a creeping discomfort. 'Go back to bed, Arella,' she said, stepping towards her with menace.

Arella stood firm as her eyes bore into Madison.

Madison laughed. 'What is wrong with you?' she said, glancing back at Selina behind her.

Selina shrugged before Madison noticed her eyes widen in surprise. She looked back at Arella and gasped. 'Shit,' she mumbled.

Arella's eyes rolled back in her head and her hands gripped the sides of the door frame as she trembled violently. Her hair bounced like a bobbin with the uncontrollable quaking of her body and a light humming emanated from deep within her throat.

'Arella?' Madison reluctantly stepped closer to the girl.

Her breath paused when Arella's shaking stopped as suddenly as it had begun. Her eyes were squeezed tightly together.

'Arella?' she repeated.

She almost lost her footing when Arella's eyes flew open. She caught herself, grasping a blood smeared hand to her chest. 'Geez, you are one spooky kid,' she laughed.

Arella's scanned her before settling on her face. 'You silly wench! Hellfire, the devil and all evil are your very own morbid conception. You give too much power to ideas that don't serve you. Evil will fail to exist when mankind ceases to give power to it,' she stated.

Her voice sounded exotic and foreign to the tongue of a little girl. 'God created man free and man has gone on to create evil, hell, disease and the devil. Judgement is not a trait of God, nor is anger or damnation to so called

sinners. This is an ego-driven deity created by humans –
man-devised rules that cast judgement over their broth-
ers and sisters to control through orthodox beliefs. It is
not too late for you to accept the authentic love available
to you. Open your eyes to the truth. We are all fuelled by
the same spark of life. There is no man better, nor lesser.
We are all from one source.'

Madison's face contorted with disbelief as something unfamiliar stirred within her. She grimaced as it
prickled up her spine like a thorny vine. Arella's eyes
appeared to shine like bright blue bulbs that penetrated
right through her.

'Arella?' she whispered.

Arella's chest grew as she took a deep breath. Her
face softened and her eyes twisted to a plea. 'The spark
of God is within you,' she murmured, before collapsing
in a heap to the floor.

'Arella!' Madison approached and stood over her.
'That was the strangest thing ever,' she mumbled as she
looked down at her.

'Whatever; just get her back to bed,' Selina huffed,
carefully stepping over Arella's body as she stalked out of
the room.

Madison gathered her up and took her back to the
bedroom. When she placed her in the bed, she gazed at
her curiously. She couldn't decide whether it was annoyance or admiration that she felt. *One thing is for sure; I*

underestimated this little brat, she mused.

'We all have our own truths, little one,' she whispered.

As she turned to leave the room, she became aware of a flickering glow permeating her consciousness.

She paused and glanced back at the sleeping girl. 'Nah,' she said with a dismissive laugh. *It couldn't be the spark of God. I'm way too ugly on the inside.*

Millie pulled on her boots and headed for the hotel door. It was still early, so she decided to walk to the cafe down the street to collect a coffee for Damon and her father. Besides, a walk in the brisk morning air would do her good. They had a big day ahead of them. Today she intended to find her daughter.

Her thoughts turned to Bella's call the night before. It's funny how someone could step into your life and somehow play such a pivotal role. Try as she had, she had been unsuccessful in her quest to find the gates of the Golden World. Samantha had told her it was because she was trying too hard, and in doing so, she was unable to expand her consciousness enough to allow the experience to unfold.

A fleeting smile played over her lips. She was

grateful that Bella could find her daughter in the other realm. She knew it was worth further pondering once this was finally over with Ace.

When Millie arrived back at the hotel some twenty minutes later, she was surprised to see Bella and Craig pulling up in a white hire car.

Bella rushed from the car towards her. 'Oh, thank God you're still here. I was worried we might have been too late,' she fretted.

Millie motioned with the tray of coffee she was holding. 'Just about to wake up the guys. I told you not to come.'

'I know, but I had to.' Bella glanced at Craig coming up next to her. 'Besides, I have brought protection,' she laughed.

'Yeah, I'm just the meat-muscle over here,' he winked, leaning to kiss Millie's cheek.

Millie grinned. 'Thanks you two,' she said. A surge of emotion rippled through her. She jiggled her head slightly to push aside the tears pooling behind her sunglasses. 'Come on, let's get this going, shall we?'

Scanning the Mary Valley map, they decided to split up into two teams to cover more ground. Luckily, Craig had brought along two Nokia handsets from his office so they could easily keep in touch with each other. Bella insisted on accompanying Millie. It was determined that Millie, Bella and Damon would ride together, leaving Glen and Craig to sift through the opposite towns of the valley.

They strode with determination towards the hotel car park.

'You know the deal, keep in touch,' Millie called, as Craig and Glen opened the car doors.

She spun on her heels to catch up with Bella and Damon. Her mind clouded with apprehension as she speculated about the coming events. She was so lost in thought that she failed to hear the screeching tyres of a car as it throttled down the lot towards her.

A loud shrill filled the air as Bella shouted at her. Millie was momentarily bewildered. *What is she scream-ing about?* Her father lunged at her. He gave her a hard shove and she found herself propelled through the air at astounding speed. *Who knew her father was so strong?* She hit the bitumen with a rolling thud, coming to a halt at Damon's feet.

She grabbed for Damon's hand and hauled herself up. She flung herself around. 'Dad!' She ran towards him, vaguely hearing the car continue its screeching exit.

Glen was lying still on the road. Blood gushed from a head wound and his clothes were frayed. Large gash-es revealed more bloody wounds over his arms and legs.

Craig was already crouched over him and calling for an ambulance.

'Dad ... dad?' Millie sobbed, falling to her knees beside him. She fumbled to rip off her cable cardigan and swathed it over his head wound.

Glen crooked his head in her direction. It took him a moment to focus and he squinted against the sun when his eyes found her. 'Millie, thank God you're okay,' he said.

She sighed with relief. 'Hey, my head wound isn't quite as bad as yours,' she said, pointing at her grazed face. 'I'm okay, thank you.'

He winced. 'Looks like I'll be stepping out of this one. I'll be fine; you go get our girl,' he said.

She nodded and gave his hand a squeeze while sirens rounded the corner to the hotel car park. 'I will. I love you,' she said solemnly, fighting the flood of tears that threatened to engulf her.

'I love you too, Millie-pie. I'm sorry,' he said. A lone tear fell from the corner of his eye and trickled over the side of his cheek.

The shrilling sirens died as an ambulance and a police car pulled up alongside them. Millie stepped back as the paramedics rushed to Glen's side armed with medical gear and a stretcher.

As the paramedics loaded Glen into the ambulance, she fought the tremor in her fingers with grim resolve. It was while they hastily gave their statements to the police that Millie began ponder whether she had been the driver's target. *Maybe this was no accident!* A chill ran down her spine. She fell against Damon's warm chest and tried to quell her suspicions.

She looked up at him. 'What now?' she said.

His face was awash with concern. 'Now we stick together. Let's go,' he instructed.

She was in no frame of mind to argue.

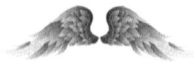

It was an hour later when they pulled into a spot in front of a small grocery store near Gympie. Bella gave her legs a stretch after being cramped in the back seat of the car. She glanced at Millie. The usual fullness of her lips had deflated into a grim line and her grazed forehead beaded with distilled blood.

'You okay?' she said.

Millie came up beside her. 'Can you think of anything else from your dreams?' she asked.

'That's all she said ... but,' she stammered.

'But what?' Millie pressed.

She shrugged. 'It's probably nothing, but last night I had another dream. There were mountains ... and I know this sounds weird, but I could smell fire.'

They both turned towards the mountain ranges behind them.

'Fire?' Millie said.

She nodded. 'The kind of fire rich with ironbark; it was so strong ... I ... I don't know if it's connected. There was some kind of a dusty arena style structure. That's all I remember.'

'Well, it's better than nothing. Let's go ask around for that arena,' she said. She turned to Damon and Craig. 'We'll take the grocery store. Why don't you guys try that cafe across the street while you pick us up a coffee?'

Bella noticed Millie's dark braided hair brush across her back like a thick black knot as she gestured. Millie's fingers grasped and pulled at the end of her braid, and Bella was mesmerised at the tiny twirls of her fingers as they manipulated the wispy ends. Her mind began to wander.

'What?' Millie demanded.

'Huh?' she blinked, and shook her head.

Millie screwed up her face at her. 'You're looking at me kind of strange,' she said.

She felt herself blush. 'Oh, I didn't mean to ... I ... Millie there is something I need to tell you. That's why I came here; well that and to help find Arella,' she said. *Oh great, I sound like an idiot*, she chastised herself. She grabbed the ends of her hair and twirled furiously.

'Well, it will have to wait,' Millie said grimly. She

grabbed her arm and tugged. 'Let's go.'

When they entered the grocery store, the old man behind the counter regarded them sceptically. He chewed on a permanently wedged toothpick while beady eyes bore into them.

Millie smiled as she approached him. 'Hi, we are looking for some kind of arena. Do you know of any around here?' she asked politely.

Bella sidled up beside her. 'Or any up in the mountain towns?' she added.

His lips worried at the toothpick, his bushy brows creased. 'That depends on what kind of arena you're talking about,' he grumbled, gesturing towards the shopfront window. 'We have all kinds, just like you city folk,' he said.

Millie's smile froze. 'Of course you do, but we're searching for a dusty arena. Does that ring any bells?' she said.

'Argh … I dunno,' he scratched the fluffy patch of hair on his head. 'I got a bell you can both tingle around with if you like,' he leered, exposing a neat set of yellowed teeth.

Bella's eyes tapered. 'Just answer the question,' she snapped. *Dirty old man.*

He cackled loudly. 'Thought I did,' he said.

Bella fought her rising frustration. 'Listen mister, we are looking for a little girl,' she gestured towards Millie.

'*Her* little girl. She's up here somewhere with a tall blonde guy and a red-headed woman. Do you know them?' she said tersely.

His beady eyes widened. 'The witch? I heard of them, but I can't say I've had the displeasure of meeting those kind,' he said.

Bella and Millie exchanged a look.

'Where are they? Are they near an arena of some kind?' Bella's voice rose in pitch.

He grunted. 'They say she lives up on the mountain in the woods,' he said. He leaned closer and lowered his tone. 'They say she's a snake-witch … people have been killed up here by snakes … strange things are happening around here.'

'Is the arena in the mountains?' Millie pressed.

He scrutinised them before slowly nodding. 'There is a rodeo arena up there; that's where the first killing was. Best be careful if you're looking for her.'

He unfolded the edges of a worn-out map and pointed a crooked finger towards the arena's location. 'This is it here. There are some old shacks and cottages this side of the arena. I heard she's there somewhere. The other side lies the gorge; nobody for miles that way,' he rasped.

They thanked him and eagerly made for the door.

'Hey!' the man called.

Bella and Millie paused to look at him.

'I was serious about the bell I have for you to tingle, don't you worry about that!' he winked, then broke out into a fit of cackles.

Bella rolled her eyes. 'Eww,' she said under her breath.

Chapter Fifteen

ILLIE TURNED AROUND TO PEER AT BELLA and Craig in the back seat. She gripped the headrest to keep herself steady while the car negotiated the winding road as they climbed the ranges. She regarded them through her dark shades. They were practically glued to one another while their hands were knotted together firmly. 'So, when did this happen?' she sniffed.

Bella grinned. 'It's been coming,' she gushed.

Millie eyed her closely. *She looks like the cat that licked the cream*, she thought. *Oh, I don't want to go there!* She rolled her eyes and took a breath. 'Okay … so, you know he's super special, right?'

Craig sighed. 'Millie,' he uttered.

Bella smiled. 'Oh, I know he's a keeper,' she winked.

Craig turned to face Bella. 'Really? I'm a keeper huh?' he murmured, leaning towards her.

She cocked her head to one side and frowned. 'Hmmm … did I just say that out loud?' she joked.

Craig laughed. 'Too late, it's out in word-land! I heard it; Millie heard it.'

'And I heard it,' Damon piped up from the driver's seat.

Bella giggled and wrapped her arms around his neck, drawing him in for a kiss.

'Yeah, we all heard it,' Millie muttered as she glanced at Damon. She groped for the map and studied it. 'How far now?' she said to Damon.

He was about to answer when a noisy pop drowned out his voice. It was like a staccato burst echoing through the car, followed by the unmistakable clunking of a rim against the road.

He pulled the car to a stop. 'Well, I was about to say half hour,' he said, getting out of the car.

'Shit,' she muttered, stepping out and surveying the shredded tyre.

'Ah, sure did a good job on that one,' Craig remarked as he too saw the damage.

'*I* didn't do a good job on anything,' Damon scowled, heading for the boot.

He grunted while he tugged at the carpet lining in search of a spare. 'We have a jack and a spare,' he called. He poked his head towards them. 'Want to give me a hand?' he said, glaring at Craig.

'Sure,' Craig shrugged, curling his long locks behind his ears and strolling towards him.

Millie ambled down the road a little while they waited for the men to change the tyre. They were midway up the mountain with a dense undertow of bushland either side of them. In the distance she could hear the low rumbling of a steam train echoing through the valley. She glanced back at the car and sighed. She knew Bella wanted to speak to her about something important, yet she was reluctant to listen to anything right now. All she wanted was to get to her daughter; everything else would have to wait. *Arella*, she thought wistfully while toying with the bristly ends of a fern, *I'm coming soon baby girl.* Her ears pricked with the slight tingle that brushed across the back of her neck. A rustle in the undergrowth caught her attention. *What is that?* She leaned forward and peered into the thick grass, gasping when she caught sight of a black scaly body moving stealthily through the scrub. *A snake!*

She spun around and started to run. She noticed Damon hauling in the blown tyre into the back of the car. Bella stared back at her in horror.

'Millie!' she screamed, waving her arms about wildly.

She glanced sideways to spy four big black snakes scrambling towards her. Their bodies twisted against the gravel road as they silently slid along at great speed.

'Holy shit!' she cursed as she picked up her pace.

She dared not look behind her as she willed her

boots to carry her faster towards the car. She scanned the scene ahead of her. Craig had shoved Bella into the car and had begun to run towards her, while Damon was closing the boot. She shook her head and raised her palm.

'No! Craig, get in the car!' she screamed.

He blundered into her, pausing to look at the snakes that were closing in fast.

'Oh dear God, how fast can snakes run?'

He grabbed her arm roughly. 'Snakes don't run, Millie, they sliver. Hurry up!' he pushed her forward.

He crammed her into the front seat of the car and slammed the door. Bella's ear-piercing shriek reverberated through the car as he swivelled to get into the back seat and found a black scaly body lurching into the car floor.

'Argh!' He grasped the snake and flung it behind him while another curled at his foot.

Damon ran from behind the car and leaped into action with the jack crowbar, driving it through the air and clobbering the snake's tail. The reptile recoiled as he brought the crowbar down hard on its head. A high-pitched hiss issued behind Damon. He spun around as another snake struck out towards him. The crowbar rattled as it collected the snake with a resounding whack. Craig shrieked. His face contorted with pain as the last snake sank its fangs deep into the flesh beneath his jeans.

Damon throttled the snake until it eventually released its stubborn grip and withdrew into a quivering coil.

Craig moaned as he grasped at his leg and leaned into the back seat of the car.

'Oh my God!' Bella ran out of the car with a T-shirt and kneeled before him. 'Don't move! We need to stop the venom from spreading to your heart.'

She clenched the shirt between her teeth and ripped at the material until it became a suitable bandage. She looked up at Damon. 'Here, hold this and pull tight when I've wrapped it.' She glanced at Millie. 'Millie, check if we have a phone signal; he needs to get to the hospital. They were red-bellied blacks; he needs the anti-venom.'

Millie nodded vaguely while reaching for the phone, and cursed under her breath. 'No signal. We have to go!' she said, her voice on the verge of hysteria.

They bundled Craig into the back seat and stretched his leg flat. Bella leaned over him. 'Don't move an inch, you hear me? Not one little bit,' she commanded.

Damon got behind the wheel. 'Buckle up, we're doing this at warp speed.' He put the car in gear and set off towards the nearest hospital.

A flock of cockatoos made a raucous chorus as Arella moaned as she stirred in her sleep. A small elbow flung over her closed eyes as the noise of the birds elevated to a shrill. Her lashes fluttered slightly as she fought to escape the deep tendrils of darkness that had enraptured her. She scuffed the top of her hair while forcing her eyes to blink open. One blink; she groaned. *My head hurts.* Two blinks; she inhaled while her eyes found the window. Three blinks; she gasped as memories of the night before flooded her mind.

A sob tore through her throat while she sat upright. Her eyes didn't leave the window as images of the fire, the knife and the lamb danced before her mind's eye. Glancing back towards the bedroom door, she strained to listen. All was quiet despite it being at least midway through the morning. She knew this by the position of the sun's rays against the only window in the bedroom. She never slept this late in the day. She figured it was because she must have bumped her head on the floor when she had fallen the night before, as it was the last thing she remembered.

Throwing the blankets aside, she tip-toed to the window. She swallowed the lump in her throat as she pulled back the curtain and peered into the yard. The winter sun beamed across the grass and warmed the forest canopy under a gentle breeze. Two white butterflies fluttered close to the window, and birds of all kinds jostled about through the air. The scene would be pleasant and inviting, if it weren't for the distinct ring of ash in the centre of the yard.

Arella's mind flashed with the haunting images of the two witches. Rosebud lips began to tremble with the pounding of her heart. She knew she had to leave this place. She had to leave now!

Scurrying to the only chair in the room, Arella pulled on a pair of worn black leggings that were too tight and an over-sized sweater. Her uncle had given her a plastic bag full of girls' clothing the day after they had arrived at the cottage. Most didn't fit properly, and all of them were used. She never asked where he had gotten the clothes, preferring not to know. Jamming her feet into her school shoes, she peeked out of the door into the tiny hallway.

There were only two bedrooms in the cottage; the other located across the hall from hers. The door to the other bedroom was slightly ajar and Arella could see the room was darkened. She sneaked into the hall and peeked into the bedroom. Her uncle was lying between Madison and Selina. Arms and legs were thrown bare and entangled over the bed, and they were sound asleep. She turned from their slumbering bodies and scampered to the front door, closing it softly behind her.

Once outside, Arella breathed in the fresh air and ignored the grumble of her empty stomach. No way was she going to chance wakening them to get something to eat. Looking left to right, a frown spread over her face as she deliberated which way to go. She decided to follow the dirt road that had taken them there, but she knew enough to keep out of sight. She knew her uncle would come looking for her as soon as he discovered she was gone.

As she set off, she spied the two butterflies she had seen through the window. They drifted closer to her and followed her as she walked down the dirt road. She smiled as a warming tingle wrapped down her spine.

'Hello butterflies. Want to go for a walk with me?' she said, pausing and holding out her hand.

They hovered in front of her before coming to rest on her palm. Their delicate wings swayed with the breeze.

She laughed softly. 'Just what I thought,' she whispered.

Ace woke with a start. A sharp breath whistled through his teeth and his eyes darted about the ceiling. For a moment he felt disoriented, then his tongue came alive as he tasted the aftermath of sex mixed with the distinct metallic zing of blood. *That was some night,* he silently applauded himself. However, his acquisition fell short as he became aware of their legs and arms splayed over him as if he were a public leaning pole.

Both women groaned when he shoved them off him and crawled out of the bed. He gazed down at them, unable to stop the rise of contempt creeping through him. Thoughts of his Softail Heritage Harley floated through his mind. He knew he needed some time with his bike and the open road; alone. And that's exactly what he intended to do after dealing with his sister.

He entered the bathroom, instantly reaching for the toothpaste and turning on the shower. The water was scalding against his skin, but he didn't care. *The hotter the better*, he thought. And reaching for the soap, he scrubbed those witches off him as best he could.

Ace wandered into the small kitchen after showering, expecting to find Arella sitting at the table doing her puzzles or drawing her next sketch for him. He loved her drawings. Each time she handed him a new one, he carefully folded the paper and stuffed it into his overnight bag. They would make good company on the road when the nights proved too still with the beating of his heart.

'Arella?' he queried. She wasn't in the kitchen or in the tiny lounge area. *Hmmm, where could she be?* He strode towards her bedroom and flung opened the door. It took only a second for his eyes to sweep the room. 'Arella?' he called a little louder. He swung around and burst through the other bedroom door. 'Where's Arella?' he boomed towards a slumbering Madison.

She sat up, rubbing her eyes while throwing off the last remnants of sleep. 'I don't know,' she said groggily.

'She's not in the cottage. Did she go to bed okay last night?' Ace growled.

She balanced herself on her hands, thrusting her bare milky breasts forward as she did so. Large straw-berry nipples poked towards him while she cocked her head to one side. 'She's probably in the garden. You were something else last night; why don't you come back and play with us, baby?' She licked her lips.

His eyes sliced through her. 'She better be,' he snarled, turning from her. *She better be.*

Chapter Sixteen

ILLIE BARELY NOTICED THE ENDLESS ROLLING hills with a landscape of patchwork littered with grazing cattle as they drove onwards. Nor did she notice the passing macadamia farms and lush rainforest as they climbed towards their destination again. Her stomach was tight and knotted. She had never believed in coincidences, but two life-threatening events on the same day that they searched for Arella proved too much a correlation. Something else was at play here, and she had a niggling feeling that that 'something else' might have to do with the witch.

Damon caressed her arm. 'Are you okay, Millie-pie?' he said.

Her eyes swung from the window to linger on him. For the first time that day she noticed how tired he looked. She covered his hand with her own and gave him a squeeze. 'I'm okay. Are you?'

He tore his eyes from the road to glance at her. 'I'll be better when we get our girl back safely.' His voice trembled.

'We're almost there! Look, there's a sign for the rodeo,' Bella leaned her head between them from the back seat.

Millie sighed audibly. *Thank God!* she thought, eager to do something more constructive than take members of their group to the hospital.

Craig had ushered them from the emergency room as soon as they had arrived at Gympie hospital. And with the staff assuring them of his wellbeing, they had left minutes later. Still, it was going on 3pm now and the sun would soon be falling beyond the horizon.

Damon steered the car along a pot-holed dirt road that opened out onto an empty car lot. Rickety timber grandstands bordered a dusty arena, and to the far side was an old brick building and a set of stables and ringed fences for livestock. The place was deserted.

Millie turned to Damon and Bella. 'Be careful out there,' she cautioned before unbuckling and getting out of the car.

She wandered to the arena and leaned against the wooden fencing. A thousand hoof marks indented the dirt like polka dots. She imagined how this place would come alive and attract a lot of locals with the excitement of rough stock events. *Giving my brother the perfect opportunity to practise his shape-shifting skills*, she shuddered.

'Millie! Bella!' Damon called from the far side of the arena.

Her heart skipped a beat. She ran to him, fighting to

catch her breath when she came up beside him. 'What is it?' she panted.

He pointed into the bush. 'There's a pathway, and listen,' he whispered, looking at her. 'I hear something.'

Arella hummed a tune as she ambled down the dirt road. She tried to ignore the dryness of her throat as she paused her song to swallow imaginary saliva. *Why didn't I at least bring some water?* she fretted, looking up towards the sun. It had moved a lot since she had left the cottage; she was certain she had been walking for hours. Granted, there had been some delightful distractions along the way. What with the butterflies and the birds and the colourful flowers; and to her joy, she had even spotted a deer prancing through the rainforest.

She stopped as a low rumbling sound caught her attention. It sounded like a gurgling stream.

'Water!' she whirled around to peer into the bush. *Should I leave the road and search for the stream?* she thought. Trying to swallow again, her tongue stuck to the roof of her mouth as she was urged forward. She peered closer into the green foliage and caught sight of a giant frog springing through the undergrowth. It was green and stripy and appeared to be heading towards the sound of the water.

Then she heard the deep grumbling roar of a motorbike closing in fast. All hesitation dissolved as a shriek escaped her lips and she dived into the bush after the frog. She knew the giant frog would lead her to the water.

Pulling the Harley to a halt at the end of the dirt road, Ace peered down the crossroads. *Surely, she couldn't have got this far?* He sighed. I guess that depends on what time she had left the cottage. He cursed himself for sleeping in so late. Usually he was up at the crack of dawn and stretching on his rock ledge over the gorge, but by the time he had arrived back from Warren Glassop's homestead the night before, it had already been late. Then Madison and Selina had kept him occupied till the early hours of the morning and time had been lost to him.

He contemplated going to Warren's homestead in search of Arella, but the thought evaporated as quickly as it had emerged. He doubted she would have gone down that way or even reached that far on foot. Besides, Warren's bantering and warning him about Madison the night before was more than an earful for him right now. The man was convinced she was responsible for

the snake deaths. His mouth twisted at the irony of that scenario.

He considered each road in turn. One led to the rodeo arena while the other connected with the main road down to Gympie. *What to do?* He shook his head. It was useless to search for his niece like this; he needed his extra sensory powers to track her scent. There was only one thing he could do.

He muttered under his breath while he gave the throttle a sharp jolt of fuel. His patience was growing thin. He had no time for this fiasco because with each passing hour he could sense his sister's presence drawing closer, and he needed to prepare for her visit.

He turned the bike and skidded over the road, leaving a brown cloud of dust in his wake as he gunned towards the arena.

Bella's eyes met Millie's. 'It sounds like running water,' she said.

Damon pulled the map from his pocket and unwrinkled the flimsy paper. 'It's the river. And look, the trail may lead to the cottages the man told you about,' he said, poking his finger at the map.

Millie sighed and looked at the trail disappearing

into the trees. She needed more than a map. She whirled around to face Bella. 'We need the angels to guide us to Arella,' her eyes pleaded. 'We need help. Are you up for it?'

Bella grinned. 'That's why I'm here.'

She about to say something to Damon but suddenly clamped her jaw shut. There was nothing more she could say to prepare him. He would just have to draw his conclusion from his observations.

The sun struck low, casting glittering rays that beamed across the tree canopy. Bursts of light flickered over them with the gentle sway of the leaves. Millie noted the sun rapidly sinking towards the horizon and inhaled sharply. Her face wrinkled with uncertainty. 'I'm not sure if this is going to work,' she said.

Bella tilted her head at her. 'Hey, I believe in you.' She caressed Millie's arm gently and lowered her voice. 'Millie with her coloured wings. You are a descendant of the angels; believe in yourself. Believe in me.'

Millie's heart cascaded with pure love like a brimming river. Her eyes filled with tears and she nodded. 'Okay,' she whispered, reaching for Bella's hands.

Their fingertips brushed together with a shimmering spark. A small smile played over Millie's lips before she closed her eyes and firmly grasped Bella's hands. The intent was powerful and they were instantly bathed in a shaft of golden light. As they focused their thoughts on one another, the golden light glimmered with a tinge of radiant pink. Her breathing slowed while she allowed herself to become immersed in the love-stream with Bella, and when she opened her eyes, she was overwhelmed at the grace and beauty of Bella's soft pink wings.

A foreign tide of knowledge flowed into her, filling the corners of her mind like a consuming tidal wave. All at once, she knew of Bella's loss and sorrow as her experiences and feelings became part of her. Her heart ached for her new friend. Emerald eyes traced over Bella's features, gradually taking in her chiselled chin against her high cheekbones and the slight prominence of her nose. Her long lashes tickled together over closed eyes, and in that moment she appeared serene and peaceful. *But there is something else.* Millie concentrated and shook her head. *Arella. Where is Arella?* She was aware of a growing sense of water. The moist substance gushed and spewed through her mind until it overflowed her consciousness. Bella's eyes flew open and peered into hers. She gasped and her jaw fell open as a flood of recognition gripped at the core of her heart.

'Millie ... Millie,' Damon's voice echoed through the radiance.

Bella's eyes held hers and she beamed towards her.

'Millie! Bella!' Damon's calls became urgent.

Millie heard the distinct rumbling sound of a

motorbike drawing near. She released her hold on Bella and the golden-pink light diminished in a gradual fuse. 'I'm sorry about your mum,' she said.

Bella's eyes glistened. 'And I'm sorry about Emily,' she whispered back.

Millie's eyes glazed over for moment. 'I …' she struggled to find the words that reflected the revelations she had experienced.

'I have a feeling you'll both be more sorry if we don't do something now!' Damon barked, gesturing towards the motorbike engine growing louder by the second.

She whirled around to face him. 'It's Ace; he's coming! But I know where she is, let's go!' she turned and stepped onto the track in the bush.

Damon and Bella followed her.

'By the way, that was some kind of awesome,' Damon mumbled behind them.

Ace circled the parking lot like a cagey predator. His eyes narrowed beneath his sunglasses when he spotted a lone car parked at the far side of one of the grandstands. The car had a sticker on the back window indicating a hire car company.

A burning spasm shuddered through his head

while he killed the bike engine and stalked around the car. Inside were a few idle belongings but nothing he recognised. He pulled his leather jacket over his gloved fist and glanced around the empty lot before slamming his hand through the passenger window. The glass burst with a loud crunch, and small chunks scattered over his boots and spilled into the front seat of the car.

He hauled the door open and grabbed the small canvas bag laying on the passenger floor. He fingered the bag before pulling it up under his nose. His nostrils flared and his eyes closed as he breathed in her unmistakable musky scent. *She smells just like her*, he sneered inwardly, sucking in more of the odour. A shadowy world began to permeate him with every intake of breath, until he could no longer tolerate the stench emanating from the duffle bag.

A beastly growl coursed through his throat as he flung the bag across the dirt road. A menacing pain shot through his head and his vision became hazy. His legs buckled and he fell to his knees while gripping his temples and howling through the empty lot. Images of Millie teased his mind as hatred twisted and overwhelmed him.

The haze in his head dissolved to reveal a set of bright yellow eyes leering at him from under the shadows of the grandstand. His coiling mind unfurled as he blinked and focused on Apepsis.

'The time has come to complete the last of your

trials, my apprentice. Once it is done, all resistance will dissolve with the puddle of blood she will leave behind, and you will finally be free of the torment that plagues you,' hissed the voice of the serpent.

Ace felt clarity pinching through his veins and pulsating with the beat of his heart. An elongated forked tongue protruded from the serpent's mouth and fondled the top of Ace's head before shrinking back between his sharp pointed fangs.

A low snigger emanated from beneath the bleachers. 'Go now and prepare for your finale. My pride, my joyous human-serpent, power and riches await you,' he sneered, before fading from sight.

Ace rose to his feet and straddled his bike with steely determination. He pulled his sunglasses into place and grinned with menace. He gave the engine a burst of fuel with the flick of his wrist before putting the bike into gear and roaring from the arena.

He knew what he had to do, and despite his recent feelings of confusion, there was no stopping him now.

Power and riches awaited.

Chapter Seventeen

CAREFUL TO KEEP HER SHOES DRY, ARELLA squatted at the edge of the river and cupped her hands. She shivered while she scooped and drank the icy cold water. After a few mouthfuls, she turned to look at the giant frog sitting on a small boulder beside her.

She wiped at her chin with her forearm. 'Thank you very much, frog,' she smiled.

The frog's sagging throat moved but no sound came nor did it acknowledge her.

'Hmmm … well, I guess I should keep going. It's going to get dark soon and I don't want to get lost in the bush in the night-time,' she said, rising to her feet.

She took a step and stopped abruptly when she heard rustling among the thick undergrowth of the rainforest. A flock of cockatoos glided overhead, screeching as their wings took them away. Her feet anchored into the moist gravel and her body stiffened as she waited for the noise of the birds to abate. She stifled a squeal as the rustling and the snapping of branches grew nearer.

He's coming for me! She looked around furiously for a suitable hiding place as she caught sight of a looming shadow through the trees. *I can't go back to those witches!* Her thoughts scattered as she eyed a big rock at the water's edge and scampered behind it.

Panic gripped her like a terrified mouse awaiting discovery. She held her breath and listened over the sound of the flowing current. All was quiet. She spotted the giant frog leaping towards her.

'Shoo! Go away!' she whispered.

The frog's legs jerked and it took another leap closer.

She was about to issue another warning to the frog when she heard the sound of footsteps in the clearing by the river. She clamped a palm over her mouth and her eyes almost popped out of her head.

A deep croak erupted from the frog and it sprang violently towards her, landing at her feet. Its bulging eyes looked up at her and it croaked again.

Arella's pulse buzzed like a whirling bee as a pair of black boots tramped over mushy leaves and pebbles until they halted beside her. She squeezed her eyes shut, not daring to peer into her uncle's face. She knew he wouldn't be happy with her.

'Oh Arella!' her mother's voice cried as she scooped her into her arms.

'Mummy, it's you!' she wailed. She gripped Millie

with a flood of relief and began to sob.

Millie smoothed her hair while she cradled her. 'It's okay butterfly. I'm here now; I'm here now,' she crooned, wiping at her tears.

Arella looked up into her mother's eyes. 'How did you find me out here?'

Millie grinned. 'I had a little help,' she confessed, gesturing towards Bella and Damon who were waving at her.

Arella leaped from Millie's arms and rushed to Bella. 'I knew you would remember meeting me in the Golden World; thank you!' She pressed her cheek against Bella's.

'Thank you for trusting me, Arella,' Bella whispered.

They exchanged hugs and Arella looked wide-eyed at Damon.

She pulled away from Bella and turned to him with a shy smile. 'You're my daddy?'

He bent to kneel before her and nodded while drinking in her image. 'You are just perfect,' he choked. He cleared his throat and extended a hand. 'I am your daddy; it's so, so good to meet you, Arella.'

A cry billowed through the air as she ignored his outstretched hand and threw herself into his arms. 'I have dreamed of you a thousand times!' she whimpered, nuzzling against his chest.

Silent tears fell over his cheeks and he closed his eyes as he held his little girl for the first time. 'I love you,' he whispered in her ear.

'I know,' she murmured.

Ace pulled the Harley to a halt outside the cottage and burst through the front door. His eyes flicked back and forth as he took in the scene in the tiny living area. He could hear Madison busying herself in the kitchen while Selina had made herself at home on the sofa.

She casually looked at him as she lay languidly like a cat. 'Well, well. Look who's finally come back. Did you find your prey?' she swung her long legs into a seated position.

He grunted at her and turned towards the kitchen.

'Hey, I was talking to you, mister!' she called.

He paused to look her way.

She smiled and pushed out her chest. 'You didn't mind giving me your attention last night,' she purred, toying with the tips of her blonde hair.

He followed her fingers as they traced over her breasts. He noticed the strain of her nipples against the flimsy blouse as they responded to her touch. He felt the desire surging through his groin, and for a moment considered a rerun of the night before. He was beside her in a flash and reaching under her blouse for a nipple. He

squeezed and bent his head for a taste while she groaned.

His mind felt numb and void as he began to gently suckle. When he closed his eyes, images of Millie and his mother burst into his consciousness. Rage skulked and stifled every corner of his mind while his suckling gave way to a savage fusion.

Selina yelped and pushed at his head. 'Stop!' she cried, shoving at him as hard as she could. She gouged a finger in his eye, forcing him to recoil.

Ace gripped her thighs and threw back his head, exposing sharp white fangs. He began to chuckle wildly before abruptly stopping, glaring back into her eyes with deep metallic blue orbs.

'Maybe later,' he sneered, standing up to cast an eye over Madison who had been watching the interaction from the kitchen threshold. 'We have company. You two stay here.'

Madison's face brightened as Ace stormed out the door, missing the grin that reflected his own on Selina's lips.

Chapter Eighteen

'WE HAVE TO GET ARELLA TO THE CAR AND out of here.' Millie grasped her daughter's hand and tugged. She could feel her brother's wrath circling through the rainforest. They didn't have long.

Damon and Bella started for the track back to the arena.

Arella pulled her arm free. 'Wait!'

All eyes turned to her.

She looked at Millie. 'I can feel him too, and I know he's not happy, but I know he's not well either.' Her dark hair tumbled over her shoulders as she shook her head. 'If we go back to the arena and leave now, the dark force will consume him completely. He needs us, mummy. I love him and he needs you.'

Millie swallowed hard before releasing an exaggerated sigh. She knew Arella was right, and she wasn't entirely sure they would make it back to the arena before he caught up with them. For all she knew, he could

already be coming down the same track as they had.

'Okay, which way then?' she said.

'Follow me,' Arella said, slipping into the rainforest.

They tramped through the bush in silence, following Arella like a small army of ants preparing to find their prize. Millie's heart thumped against her ribs while she negotiated the dense undergrowth. The emotions that coursed through her were not of the prize-winning kind. She was uncertain of what to expect and even more unclear of her abilities to banish the darkness from her brother's soul. She took a deep breath as she began to focus her thoughts on Ace, initiating the cleansing process by envisioning him bathed under a stream of ultraviolet. The violet ray represented mercy and compassion along with forgiveness as she knew it was forgiveness his soul craved to regain its freedom.

Shadows loomed through the rainforest ahead, and the light was fast diminishing. A few more turns and they stepped from the thicket of trees and vines onto a huge sandstone ledge overlooking a deep gorge.

'This is his special place,' Arella said. 'He comes here every morning and connects with his surroundings.' Her arms spread in a wide gesture. 'I think you will have a better chance of reaching him here.'

Damon skirted the edge and peered into the gorge. 'Whoa! Are you sure about this?'

Millie came up beside him and gazed down at the

steep narrow valley. The hard stone walls plunged down to the streaming river below. She might have soaked in the magnificence of the view and marvelled at its raw beauty any other day, but not this time.

A terrified shiver shimmied down her spine. 'I guess it will have to do. The sun is about gone,' she shrugged.

A high-pitched hiss echoed up through the trees and filled the valley. Arella gasped. 'He's coming!'

Millie spun around in search of a suitable hiding place. Her eyes settled on a giant cluster of shrubs to the far side of the sandstone and away from the cliff edge. 'Take her away, and stay with her. Both of you!' She pointed to the shrubs.

'But …'

'Millie …'

'No, mummy!'

Millie remained firm. 'Go! He's my brother. He knows me and loves me. You won't be far if I need you,' she insisted, struggling to keep her voice even.

Another hiss issued from the rainforest. They flew into action. Millie hid behind a boulder on the opposite side of the shrubs where Damon and Bella had taken Arella. The last of the sun's rays cast vivid blood-orange streaks across the horizon and she could barely make out the shrubs on the far side of the cliff now. *Good*, she thought, while attempting to calm the gush of blood rushing through her veins.

Leaves rustled and crunched from the bush behind her. She caught her breath as she felt the little fine hairs on the back of neck poise in alert. Her heart hammered as she turned her head slowly to come face to face with large slitted sapphire eyes glowing at her from a sea of darkness.

A raspy voice taunted her from the gloom. 'Nobody loves me; everybody hates me. Think I'll go eat ... angels.'

Her teeth seized her bottom lip and every inch of her stiffened except the repeated blinking of her eyes. Was this her brother?

The serpent's mouth widened in a smirk as he revealed himself. 'Hello dear sister,' he sniggered.

She backed away, bumping against the boulder behind her while her eyes shifted around, evaluating her options. He was so close she could smell the foul stench of his breath as a warm draft wafted over her with each exhale of his lungs. She knew she wouldn't be quick enough to escape a powerful strike.

'Ace, is that you?' She fought the quiver in her voice.

A harsh chuckling issued from his throat. 'Tell me, have I grown since you've seen me last? Have I changed that much?' His laughter continued.

Clearly, he was amused.

'Stop that!' she fumed.

He chuckled louder, sounding like a crazed madman.

Millie stamped her foot into the earth. 'Ace, this is not who you want to become. This is not the real you! I know who you are; do you remember me? Remember how close we used to be and the times we laughed together until we cried?' Her eyes pleaded with him as she tripped over her words. 'Remember how I made you feel? Happy. I made you feel happy. You can be happy again.'

Ace fell silent while he contemplated what she had said. 'I remember how you betrayed me when you brought my mother back from death,' he sneered, flaring his forked tongue at her.

She cringed as the tip of his tongue hovered in front of her face. 'Ace, please ... I love you,' she whispered.

His fleshy tongue shrunk back. Mammoth fangs glistened like dripping icicles as he twisted his scaly head while his eyes devoured her as if she were a hamburger. Jaws the size of a great white shark thrust towards her and she squeezed her eyes shut as she flinched for a puncturing impact.

She felt her body jerk suddenly as Damon's hands grabbed her arms and tackled her sideways. Together they tumbled in a tangle, bashing into the ground with a loud smack. She whirled her eyes around in time to witness the serpent's jaws clash together with driving strength.

Ace adjusted his head to face them. His eyes gleamed with insane rage as his scaly wrapped muscles flexed fiercely.

Already on his feet, Damon gallantly stood between them while Millie scampered to regain her footing behind him. 'Ace! It's me, Damon!' he yelled desperately.

A flicker of recognition sailed through his eyes. Ace paused for the briefest of moments before lifting his long body and violently thrusting himself through the air with a throaty roar. The back of his head smashed into Damon's thigh and a loud crack sounded as he was flung like a ragdoll into the darkness of the bush.

'Damon!' Millie screamed, pivoting on her feet to run after him.

Ace lashed his tail, propelling himself between them. 'You can't escape me, Millie. No-one can save you now,' he hissed.

Millie shut her eyes and forced herself to find her centre of consciousness. She levelled her breathing and began to summon the white light. 'God! Creator of everything. Requalify his soul with your light until all darkness is consumed,' she shouted repeatedly.

A subtle ray appeared and drifted over her like a luminous cloud.

Ace began to laugh. 'Still as stubborn as ever, I see,' he jeered. 'I told you no-one can save you, not even the source of creation.'

'Even God needs a little help from time to time, brother!' Bella's voice boomed between them as she joined Millie and turned to him.

Ace poised before them like a cobra. 'I thought I could smell another … yet your scent is so like hers,' he said.

Bella gave a half laugh and grasped Millie's hand. 'She is my twin and I am your sister,' she said.

She shut her eyes alongside Millie and her chest rose visibly as she entered the white ray and became one with the shield of light. Pink, violet and golden hues interlaced above them as the divine healing rays bubbled and danced until they were fully bathed in them. Their opaque wings appeared and lingered behind them in a graceful poise while they directed the love-stream to their brother.

Ace squirmed and tossed his elongated body under the rich glow as Millie and Bella approached him. They stood to either side while their wings spread in a colourful spectacle to encompass his decrepit scaly form. Each of them directed a stream of celestial light into his heart, filling every beat with love and forgiveness until they could no longer feel the evil resistance lurking in his soul.

Arella's petrified squeal shot through their consciousness like a cutting blade. 'Mummy!' she bellowed.

It took a moment for Millie's eyes to adjust, and

when they did she gasped when she saw Madison holding Arella with a knife blade against her throat.

'Arella!' she yelled, advancing towards them.

Madison tightened her grip. 'Back away! Let Ace be, and you can have her,' she cried. Her dark eyes nervously darted to Ace. 'Come on, baby!'

Millie's heart dropped when she glanced at her brother. He slowly uncurled his black body and his sapphire eyes glistened at her. Failure clutched at her soul and snatched her breath like a whipping tornado. *It didn't work, he's still a serpent!* Her eyes misted up.

Madison shifted on her feet and blew tassels of hair from her face. 'Hurry up my serpent. Apepsis awaits you!' she urged.

Millie took another step, freezing when she saw Madison twisting the knife against Arella's throat.

'Please don't hurt my baby!' she wailed.

Arella yelped as the tip of the blade cut through her flesh and blood trickled down her neck like an oozing fountain pen. She gulped visibly and the tremble of her little body stiffened. Her eyes became wide as saucers as she watched her uncle slither towards them.

Millie watched helplessly. 'Ace, please … no!' she begged.

Her body quaked while she dropped to her knees and felt Bella's arms come around her. She clasped at her face and desperately called for her daughter.

'That's my niece, you dirty witch!' Ace roared.

A high-pitched scream echoed through the night. Millie lifted her eyes to see Arella running towards her as Ace sunk his fangs deep into Madison's flesh. He lifted Madison up in his jaws and flung her body off the side of the cliff into the gorge below.

Silence hung in the air like a heavy cloak while Millie's racing heart matched that of her daughter's as she held her close and squeezed tightly.

She turned to Bella, gently stroking her hand. 'Thank you,' she whispered.

Bella smiled. 'Thank you, sister,' she said softly. 'I'm going to find Damon.'

Millie nodded and looked for Ace, yet he was no longer where she had last seen him.

'Ace,' she called, rising to her feet.

She winced with the pain that began to swell through her joints while searching around the sandstone and calling his name. Her attention was momentarily captured by an iridescent light emanating from the bush. She grinned. *Bella is getting the hang of this*, she thought, turning around to peer into the inky shadows again.

A tall figure emerged out of the darkness, and as the figure drew closer, an electric tingle ran up her spine and drifted over her head.

'Ace?' she murmured.

'Millie-pie,' he said uncertainly.

Tears stung her eyes as he stepped closer and held her gaze. A smile spread over her lips as she recognised the sky-blue of his eyes had replaced the blazing sapphire of recent years. He smiled back at her before pulling her close and embracing her.

'I love you too,' he whispered.

'Does anyone happen to have any chocolate around here?' Bella piped, coming up behind them.

Millie laughed through her tears as she turned to look at Damon, Bella and Arella. She slung her arms around them all. 'I love you guys,' she said.

No-one noticed the two sets of slitted yellow glowing eyes watching them through the murky trees, nor Selina as she turned and quietly slinked away.

Epilogue

September 7, 1998

Dear Journal,

A lot can happen in three weeks. For instance, it was exactly three weeks ago that I had planned on introducing father and daughter over a special home-cooked dinner only to find she had been kidnapped by my brother, Ace.

Since then, my father was run over by a madman-driven car aiming for me, Craig was bitten by a demon-possessed snake itching to sink its fangs into my legs, and my brother revealed his shape-shifting abilities to me. Believe me when I say it wasn't the most joyful of experiences, but at least my father and Craig are back home and on the mend.

I look back now and it all seems like a dream. And speaking of dreams, I have expanded my consciousness to allow the wonderful realm of the Golden World to flow to me. Its mystical gates beckon me and I spend a great deal of my dream world frolicking among ascended beings and playing with Arella and Bella. Samantha meets with us and continues to teach us as we negotiate our paths. She is pleased with the progress of my relationship with my twin, and my father. We have joyfully embraced Bella into our family.

When we returned to Sydney, Bella handed me the letter her mother had left behind. After reading the words which explained the circumstances of our birth and separation, I knew in my heart it was the truth. Who am I kidding? I knew it was truth the day Bella had communicated it to me through the light-ray at the arena.

Damon has moved in with us too. Yes, I know it appears to be a hasty decision but life is just too precious to allow time to waste without your loved ones. Arella is tickled pink. With each passing day, her glow shines brighter as the bond with her father finds its roots.

My feature in New World Art magazine was released last week. Since then, Damon has been overwhelmed with exhibition offers, numerous bids for features, and most importantly, my canvases have tripled in price almost overnight! Miss Grey called to inform us that apparently, she had some reliable inside knowledge that the White House planned to send Richard Holbrooke to Kosovo next month to negotiate a peace deal. She is certain it has something to do with my paintings hanging among the presidential walls.

I can only smile as we make plans to visit New York _ and I negotiate my final ascension into the light.

And as for Selina, no-one has seen or heard from her since our recent ordeal. Sometimes, I get an eerie feeling the serpent still lingers near. But when I gaze at my brother and look for the signs in his eyes, the peace I find there stills my restlessness.

With the wings of an angel firmly behind me, I leave you with a copy of Rose's letter.

In Love, Faith, Charity and Healing,

Millie xo

Dear Annabella,

Your father and I used to say you were are a gift from the angels. There is more truth to those words than you are aware. You see, you are the daughter of my own daughter. She came to us gifted and embodied from the divine legion of Ascended Angels, chosen to come to earth and intervene with the deadly wrath of Apepsis.

While she loved your father, Samantha knew it would not be her lifetime to heal and eradicate the dark force within him, but their offspring that would regenerate his soul. Yet when she discovered she carried twins, her own guiding angel insisted that one of you would remain absent from his awareness and raised without the dark influence shadowing the baby's life. So it was done; the reaches of the Ascended Angels really has no bounds, and it wasn't so hard to conceal your birth from your father.

It was believed your upbringing would be pure and coupled your sister's contrasting experience, therefore give you and Millie's uniting powers a higher level of consciousness. That way, your path for success in conquering the serpent would be assured.

I am overjoyed she has come into your life before my final calling, and please forgive me for keeping this vital truth from you for so long. Alas, timing is everything.

I will love you forever Wonder-Bella.
Mum

Connect with Kim

Website: www.kimpetersen.com.au
Facebook: www.facebook.com/kimpetersen11
Twitter: www.twitter.com/kimpeace.com

Other titles in this series:
Millie's Angel
A Stroke of Faith: A Novelette

Sign up to hear more from Kim Petersen and get your free novelette!

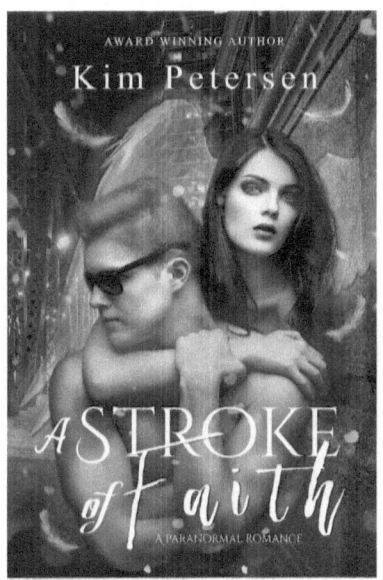

www.kimpetersen.com.au/join-whispers-.html

About the Author

ROBERT V. FRIEDENBERG is Professor of Communication at Miami University, Ohio. Among his most recent publications are *Communication Consultants in Political Campaigns* (Praeger, 1997) and *Political Campaign Communication* (Praeger, 2000, 4th edition).